by Theodora Koob

SURGEON'S APPRENTICE

BENJY BRANT: DRAGOONING WITH THE SWAMP FOX

BENJY BRANT

Dragooning with the Swamp Fox

BENJY BRANT

Dragooning with the Swamp Fox

by Theodora Koob

ILLUSTRATED BY LEONARD VOSBURGH

J. B. LIPPINCOTT COMPANY · PHILADELPHIA AND NEW YORK

FIRST EDITION

Contents

CHAPTER ONE

Trouble Rides the Breeze

IT CAME quietly, at first—a whisper on the soft September breeze: the trouble. It was nothing more than wisps of pungent odor that irritated the three children teetering on the plank across the stile. At the beginning, they rubbed their noses without thinking why.

After a little while, Alice Hawley said, "Smells like something burning."

Benjy scanned the top of the woods as far as he could see, and then he looked toward the meadow and the western hills. "Don't see smoke," he stated.

"Smells like burning, even so," Alice repeated.

And it did. But the breeze kept rising and falling as an early autumn stir will do. With this fluctuation, the acrid odor came keener and then less keen and then sharp again.

"Here comes Paw," Melinda noticed presently from the peak position of the plank.

Will Brant was riding harder than usual, peeling a scatter-up of dust along the wormwood fence line from the road gate. Benjy dropped his feet into the dry dirt close to the plank end and waited, balancing the girls' level on the other side.

His father's wool shirt was open and prickles of sweat clung to the hairs on his neck. His thick brown hair was loosened from its tiestring. His skin leggings were soaked with perspiration, his own and the lathered piebald's. Normally, he never rode hard, pounding, fierce on such a hot afternoon.

"Paw?" Benjy wondered as his father reined in.

"Better go on home, Alice," Mr. Brant said bluntly to the girl. "Tell your paw I said he was right; they're burning all along below . . . reckon that we'll have 'em up here tomorrow."

Alice swung Melinda across the plank and set her on the edge of the stile. The board banged down into the soil and Benjy stood free of it. Alice Hawley caught up her kersey skirt in both fists, dropped a half curtsey in politeness, turned, and ran over the meadow and the rise.

"Why'd ye send Alice home, huh, Paw? Why?" Melinda demanded, bouncing up and down on the stile top while Benjy hauled off the plank and carried it back to set it against the loom house.

"Because," her father said absently. He was already unbuckling his saddle girth. In a moment he flung the saddle on the sward and shook the wet blanket onto the fence to dry. "Walk her some, son," he said to Benjy, who was coming back.

The boy took the reins. "What's the burnin', Paw?" he asked more practically than Melinda.

But his father didn't answer him at all; instead he asked if the sheep were in their back pasture. Benjy said they were as he began pacing their little piebald mare up and down before the stile.

"And where's your maw?"

"She's in the loom house, I b'lieve, finishin' off that piece on the frame," Benjy replied.

Will Brant began walking up and down on the opposite side of the horse with his big hands entwined behind his back and his thick brows knit. It occurred to Benjy that his father might have walked the overheated horse himself. But since Mr. Brant did not offer to speak, the boy asked no more questions.

"Why'd ye send Alice on, Paw, why?" Melinda asked twice more; then she hopped off the stile and ran toward the loom house to report to her mother.

After several trips of about thirty or forty paces up and back with the horse, Benjy noticed Aaron Hawley striding down toward the stile, his sheep dog at his heels, his wife and daughter following a bit farther behind. Alice was swinging her sunbonnet by one string. Mistress Hawley reached out and slapped at her for doing it.

As though he had quite expected the Hawleys, Will Brant stopped pacing and set one foot on the first step of the stile. Brant's dog Striker came bellowing from the pasture and stood wagging his tail and sniffing at Hawley's Bowser through the fence rails. Benjy's mother came from their loom house with Melinda and hurried to greet the Hawleys.

"Right I was?" Aaron Hawley began.

"Aye," Mr. Brant replied briefly.

"And where be they now?" Mr. Hawley asked.

"At Congers' and will stay the night, I suppose, and be to Benning's at breakfast," Mr. Brant said in a tone Benjy thought unusually sharp.

"Did you warn George Benning?"

"I did!"

"And he'll not, heh?" Aaron Hawley demanded.

Will Brant shook his head and wiped his hot face. "I know not, likely not, for he thinks like me. Todd will capitulate and McGarve not, so they'll be here by three o'clock tomorrow I expect. 'Tis not much time

"You can smell the burning true enough as Alice told," Hawley observed, wrinkling his nose.

" 'Tain't the burnin' so much as the killin'. Better keep your women in the house," Will Brant advised tartly.

"You're a fool, Will Brant, that's what . . . wi' a coming flock like yours, neat kept and thick fleeced. You're a fool, I say." Hawley's big mouth was drawn tight. "A man can easier lie than die, I say."

"You needn't say . . . for you can't feel the same way," his neighbor snapped in the unfamiliar bitter voice Benjy had noticed.

"I can put myself in your moccasins, Will!"

"No, not truly, let me be."

"If I can do aught at all, you be sendin' up," Aaron Hawley offered.

Will Brant nodded gratefully. "Keep your women in, 'tain't pretty what I saw below."

"Paw, what you all talkin' 'bout like that so solemn and church-y?" Melinda asked.

"Hush," her mother said, jerking her thick brown braids.

Aaron Hawley turned from the fence and taking his wife's shoulder, he spun her gently around toward their house. Alice put both hands on the under fence rail, made a silly face at Benjy, turned, and ran home.

"Put Bessie in the field to graze now but tether her on a halter, I ain't fixin' to chase after her tomorrow," Will Brant said; he began walking toward their cabin in short slow steps.

"Shall I finish up, Will?" Mistress Brant asked, brushing at her forehead though her soft brown hair was all tucked into her sunbonnet.

"Yes, do that; get the stuff off the loom and bring any bolts to the cabin," Mr. Brant directed.

Benjy took Bessie behind their cabin up into the first field. After changing her bridle for a halter, he tied her on a long rein beneath their catalpa tree. He plucked a huge leaf and began pressing his nail into it absently. But in a moment he threw it away and ran down to the cabin, questions grating him into anxiety.

His father was sitting at their big trencher table with the two first fingers of both hands pressed against his temples and his lips rolled in.

"Are you all right, Father?" Benjy asked, anxious immediately.

Will Brant nodded. "Aye."

"Father, what's capitulate, huh? What is't?" Benjy wanted to know.

"It's more than one thing, Benjy boy. It's somewhat like surrenderin' in a fight and again it's like givin' in against what you believe, and for a man like Don Berry whose fear rattles in his throat, it's takin' the easy way to avoid trouble," his father explained.

"What trouble, the burnin' trouble? I don't understand you, Paw, not a whit."

Will Brant nodded his rugged head and smoothed back his hair. "Aye, son, ye don't, and what ye really want to know is what Aaron Hawley meant when he said to capitulate, that's what ye want to know. Well, a detachment of king's soldiers are comin' who are asking every man of us to swear our allegiance to King George and to give up our arms and ammunition, and that's one kind of capitulation. For Aaron Hawley, 'tis the right thing to do. But for me, Benjy boy, 'tis dead wrong and I'm agin' it!"

This was a long speech for Benjy's father, who was generally short spoken though he thought deeply about things like politics and religion and good and bad ways. The boy

13

came and threw a leg over the bench on their side of the table and leaned across to search his father's face.

"So?" he asked, bidding for more information.

"I'll not lie, Benjy, I'm for the Congress and the legislature. And besides that, I'll hide my guns before they get to take 'em. We've Indians yet out here now and anon."

Silence was thick between them. Then Benjy said, "So?" again.

"For them like me, they're burnin' the loom houses and the wool and killin' the sheep! You smell the burnin'." Yes, the smell was in the house even, subtle, tangy, noticeable.

"I don't believe it!" Benjy cried. "What sense is't? What did the poor sheep do?"

" 'Tis nothing about the sheep themselves," cried Mistress Brant from the doorway where she came in with a long folded bolt of newly loomed wool, the farther end of which Melinda held up valiantly. " 'Tis to make us want, that's what! So we do as they say; and we must come to it. Can't ye see that, William Cyrus Brant?" she demanded of her husband. "Let it fall, Melly, I'll get it later," she said of the cloth.

"That may be, but I'll not give in now, and likely never . . . not while I can hunt and fish, not while the wilderness lies beyond to start over if need be . . ."

Anna-Mary Brant burst into tears. Benjy knew that she thought of the cabin building, the well digging, the back-breaking labors of clearing and planting, the long years that little Melinda could not remember at all . . . Benjy could remember when they had thanked God on their knees for every new lamb. He was well past fourteen, but Melinda was only eight and had been born in the cabin and had learned to walk beside the intricate beams and harnesses of the big loom in the loom house.

"Hush, woman," Will Brant said, but he was not unkind; it was his way and the way of their life.

"What shall we do?" Anna-Mary wondered, wringing her hands.

"We have until tomorrow, let us go on living," her husband returned practically. "Nothing can change before tomorrow afternoon. But I'll not set any more cloth." As though he just that moment noticed his son idle at the table, Mr. Brant shook a finger at him. "Get Moomoo down and milk her, 'tis time."

Benjy went up to the back pasture where the cow grazed along with the fine Brant flock of sheep. Lambs were gamboling everywhere, their mothers baaing querulously. Admiring them, Benjy thought that it couldn't be true that anyone would kill all those innocent beasts. A little waft of breeze brought the smoke smell again to his nostrils. He sought the cow. Under his gentle prodding Moomoo began to move carefully down pasture; her milk bag was so full, it made her awkward. Melly stood at the bar and pulled it loose.

"They're arguin', Maw and Paw," she advised with a tuppence smarty little girl look.

"Never mind, Missy," Benjy said. " 'Tis no simple thing, lobster-backs burnin' looms and killin' sheep all over the place."

"*I* don't believe it," Melly tossed her braids.

"To tell truth, I don't either. Want to sneak out with me, after, and see what we can find out?" he proposed.

"You know how to get through the woods?" Melly asked.

"I reckon, and 'twill be full moon. Only you'd better not whine and scare none."

Melly beamed at him; her round freckled face shone. It

wasn't often Benjy asked her along on his excursions. "I promise . . . 'n' you wake me sure if I fall asleep?"

He nodded. They prodded Moomoo gently on through the gate.

CHAPTER TWO

Sixpence Worth of Noseyness

THE BRANT attic was yet unfinished. But its farther end was permanently floored and had its own entrance up a notched log stair. Here Anna-Mary and Will Brant slept. The children in turn had slept there, too, in the trundle bed; but now they had graduated to the open end of the loft which was warmer. Unwalled, it caught the heat of the huge fireplace first. Benjy's bed was built into the wall corner right over the cabin door; Melinda's was on the farther corner. Eventually, when Will Brant had time to set a puncheon floor on the rest of the rafters, Melinda would have a room of her own.

Never had two children been more painstakingly eventempered and gentle with each other and their parents. Had Will Brant been a bit less preoccupied, he would certainly have suspected some devilment in the planning stage. Why, Melinda scraped the trenchers without being told once; and Benjy filled the woodbox to overflowing and toted the fresh milk to the spring house without more than one reminder. And never were two children so eager to go to bed! Melinda set the chairs straight, held the new spun wool for winding, willingly took a turn at the churning when Benjy went out to the sheep with his father. Without complaining, she set out a half bushel of hoed yams to dry in the next morning's sun.

Benjy came in from hobbling Moomoo and with a sharp stick retraced the floral edging his mother had designed in their clean-swept, packed dirt floor.

"Will it just never be time to go to bed?" Melinda worried in a thin whisper once.

"Hush, of course, besides 'tis not full dark nor moon-rise yet," Benjy muttered. "Be patient now or you'll give it away that we're up to't!"

At dark, Will Brant lit a fat candle and got out the Bible and opened it. He read the verse that his finger touched. He said nothing else, no other word at all. He did not even suggest that he had looked for comfort or advice. But Benjy knew his father was not a man to turn to scripture every night. Melinda's eyes grew as big as a bottle bottom in awe. And Anna-Mary swiped at her eyes with the hem of her apron. Not anyone of them made a word of comment. What Will Brant read was:

> "Take therefore no thought for the morrow;
> for the morrow shall take thought for the
> things of itself. Sufficient unto the day
> is the evil thereof."
>
> Matthew VI, 34

After several moments of heavy quiet, Mr. Brant said gruffly, "Unfold your ladder, children, and get up to bed."

Benjy took their folding ladder out of the corner behind the cupboard and sprung it open and leaned it against the loft edge. It was a tidy device, that ladder. Benjy remembered when his father had made it: how he had whittled the dowel rungs and fitted the pegs so they could be pulled to release the dowels which fit into slots. The children trotted up.

"Leave the candle handy," Melly whispered, bouncing on her cornshuck mattress.

"No need," Benjy assured her, "the moon will make it light as anything. I set my rifle handy against the sheepfold when I went out with Paw. Now you cover up and pretend asleep. Don't go hopping in and out of bed and get Maw to thinkin' things. If you go to sleep, I'll wake you, I promise." He set his shoepacks at hand and kept on his kersey breeches and his linsey undershirt.

In a very little while, both children heard their mother start up the stair on the far side of the loft. "Are you coming to bed, Will?" she called gently to her husband.

"Reckon I'll walk over to Aaron's a moment first; I'll not be long."

Benjy could hear Melly bounce in disgust, and he giggled under his hand. He listened next for the door to swing shut after his father. It seemed a long time before footsteps returned, whispering through the long grass outside the cabin; but actually Benjy knew his father had kept his word and stayed only a quarter hour or so. Mr. Brant, by the sound of his hard stride, was out of sorts. He banged the door, too, and went up immediately. He moved around a few seconds and grumbled some brief comment to his wife, who was evidently yet awake. Then everything settled into stillness.

Unable to wait until her brother made up his mind to start, Melly finally tiptoed across the space between their beds and whispered, "Maw's snorin' gentle, I can hear."

"All *right*," Benjy muttered. "You can wait on my pleasure. I thought the idea up. Do you still smell the smoke any?"

"Uh-huh, faint-y . . ."

"Don't stumble coming down, let me go first. And don't, for mercy sake, bump into anything. That would bring Father down like a shot." The boy fumbled his feet into his shoes and tied their thongs. He put on his knit jacket. "Got somethin' warm? Might be cool in the woods, you know."

"I got my wool blouse, the new one, and a muffler."

"All right, come on now, easy." Benjy led the way down the ladder and even placed Melly's feet on the first two rungs by holding her ankles. If it had been cool enough for a fire in the hearth, they could have seen the ladder better. They had to feel their way down. But they made it and got safely along the edge of the table benches around to the door. The string latch was in. Benjy loosed it without a sound and pulled the door in just enough to let Melinda squeeze through. In a moment he was after her and had eased the door closed again.

The darkness outside was sweet and cool, and the orange edge of the moon showed through the tree tops in the east like a burnished pumpkin. Benjy held out his hand as they ran toward the stile. He helped Melly over. They hustled across Hawley's front pasture because it was shorter to the woods that way. By the time they broke into the tree line, the moon was high enough to be seen in full, beckoning them on. Benjy knew myriad little paths, knew them so well that not even the darkness confused him. Once they startled a grouse that rose whirring. Once Melly stepped in a boggy place and squealed. Otherwise they seemed to be going unerringly forward toward the great shiny moon. The smell of the burning increased presently, gradually becoming thicker and more irritating as though a fire had died and was smoldering. The trees began to thin out. Suddenly they were on the edge of a meadow rising sharply into a hill.

"Where we now, Benjy, huh?" Melinda demanded.

"McGarve's I think, and on t'other side of the hill is Todd's; but we've a fur piece to go to Congers'. You tired yet?"

"Not me," she returned gallantly.

"Well, hustle then, you take such bitsy steps and 'tis more'n a whoop and a holler yet."

Melly ran awhile, almost skipping; then both children settled into a fair trot, for Benjy was beginning to feel the weight of his long rifle. They could see the pastureland plainly enough, avoiding pitfalls and rocky places. After a bit, Benjy pointed out the road running before the big double Todd cabin. As soon as the children reached the road below it, the going was easier.

"Smoke's about to choke me now," Melly observed at last, and then in a childish stage-whisper she added, "I hear something!"

They stopped to listen. Benjy set the gun down on its butt. They heard a shuffling noise, soft rustling; and it was somehow familiar. Quickly, Benjy recognized what it was, a flock of sheep moving all of a piece, guided, prodded. Sure enough, over a rise in the road, the children saw the animals huddling along, their flat faces with their anxious expressions pushing out of the herd; sheep moving in a troop always seemed to be confused, distressed. The two men who were herding them were doing it stealthily without much talk or noise.

Melinda started forward eagerly, but Benjy caught her by a braid with a harsh "Shhh! Come here. Let's get behind this hedge."

"Why? No sheep man would hurt us . . ."

"Never mind, do as I say," he dragged her with him. "Can't you figure what it is and why they're so quiet? 'Tis Benning's herd, I bet, and he's tryin' to move 'em somewhere. How can he hide a flock of sheep, I ask you?"

"Maybe you'd try if you was to lose ours, wouldn't you?" Melly said with unanswerable logic.

The sheep never quite reached the two hidden children. From across the far field came a veritable whooping and hollering, the flash of metal, a couple of pistol shots. A small band of mounted soldiers with their leader soon accosted the nearest shepherd.

"Sneaking out, were ye?" The children heard the words plainly. Frightened, they bent close to the ground though their bush was protection enough; for the last thing the British soldiers would have expected was two children alone on the roadway.

The Benning youth, if it were he, was quick enough. "Changing pastures is all, nice moonlight night," he cried. " 'Tis also my father's field yonder."

"Yea? Well, take 'em back to the field they was in, now," the officer shouted. "And await our disposition to-morrow, you hear, and we'll remember!" The word was a threat.

Benjy's blood seemed stopped thickly in his veins and he squeezed his gun as he might have squeezed the hand of his best friend. "Hush," he muttered; but Melly had no need of the warning. She was biting her teeth together.

It was some little time before the two young men turned their sheep successfully. Slowly, the herd shuffled out of sight.

"Come on," Benjy whispered finally.

"Let's go home, Benjy, I want to go home," Melly whimpered; she had had her fill of excitement.

"No, now I'm this far, I want to see what the burnin' was; that's what we came for. We're no more'n half a mile from Congers' now. Let's get on."

The soldiers had ridden back across the field from which they had come. The children kept to the road. As they passed Benning's, they noticed that the sheep were huddling around the half shelter where they would normally be most of the time. The road rose over a small hill again and then dropped down. Below lay Congers'. What had been their loom house was a blackened mass of burnt timber, still glowing angry red in spots. Benjy gripped his gun with both hands. What his father had said was true; they saw the evidence. And even more grim, the Congers women, mother and daughters, were fetching and carrying for British soldiers sitting at a big table set on saw horses in the barnyard. Food and drink the conquerors had evidently exacted. In the light of torches set into holders on stakes, the troopers were laughing and joking and making free with the food while their horses stamped nearby, rope-hobbled. The soldiers' red coats with their gold braid and black trimmings made bright patches of color in the torch and moonlight. Even the grass shone shinier green and the smoking fire more glowing red in the off-light.

"Come on," Benjy tugged at Melly's hand. "Let's sneak back around this way and see what it is with Congers' flock." He took a wide turn along the course of a fieldstone pasture fence. Carefully, following her brother's example, Melly, too, bent down below the fence level though she was hardly tall enough to be seen above it. They topped the hill, Benjy first. He dropped to his knees, threw the rifle out before him and choked into his hands. He remembered his sister.

"No, Melly! Go back down, don't look," he cried.

But it was too late; she was already there. And directly before them lay a dead lamb, its throat cut wide. All down the hillside, the sheep were dead, stabbed, horse trampled, their throats slashed—it was horrible. The children turned and ran down the hill on the side they had come up. Without thinking, they ran headlong. Of course, Benjy was tall enough to be seen. Someone gave the alarm; before they had quite reached the road, they were pursued by a tall officer who had jumped up from the end of the great table. He leaped the fence, reached out a long arm and caught Melly by her braids. Benjy did not abandon her. He stopped in his tracks, pivoted slowly, and faced the Britisher.

"So, ho! and what have we here? Running away, eh?"

"No, suh, yes, I mean," Benjy hedged. "We're not from here!" he cried out bravely. "Paw . . . Paw was mad and we just lit out."

"Did you now?" The officer didn't believe it, certainly. He beckoned to one of the Congers women who came timidly out of the circle of torch light to the edge of the stone fence. "Know this boy? Is he one of yours?"

"No, Lieutenant, I never saw him before," she said; perhaps truly, though she might have seen the Brant children at a harvest time or church fair. She was brave to deny him, anyhow, Benjy thought.

"You go armed, eh? When you run away peeved?" the lieutenant held out his hand for the gun. Benjy gripped it tighter. "Give it here, boy."

" 'Tis mine, my own, and I earned it."

"Did you?" the fellow laughed, as if the idea tickled him. "Let's say that it *was* yours. We collect this kind of thing. Bertie here needs one," he wrested the gun from the boy deftly with a clever twist that hurt both Benjy's wrists. "Hey, Bertie, give me sixpence for your long rifle now! Looks a far bargain at that price," the lieutenant shouted at a trooper.

Hot anger boiled up in Benjy's chest. He knew his face was lobster red; and he was afraid, too. He stood starkly before Melly, who was frozen with fear. The soldier named Bertie got up from the table, caught the rifle when the lieutenant flung it toward him, felt in his breeches pocket and tossed out a piece. The coin fell at Benjy's feet.

"There, pick it up, boy," the officer said. Benjy didn't move. Roughly, the British soldier reached out and snapped up the boy's head with his fist. Benjy's teeth drew blood in his lip but he made no moan. "Who are ye not to obey, eh?" Still propping the boy's head back on his fist, the lieutenant eyed him keenly. "If she doesn't remember you," he nodded toward the Congers girl, "I shall! I shall remember you. Now pick up the coin and get home with you, do't!"

Melinda had begun to shake violently. Benjy was so tense that his head and throat both ached. He had no choice either. He picked up the sixpence and caught at Melly's elbow and swung her around. They ran, hard, as hard as they could still keeping together, a lot harder than they might have expected that they could. And stinging tears began to course down Benjy's dusty face. He felt like a baby but he could not hold them back; he wept for the gun, of which he had been so proud, and for the humiliation of its price, and for not believing his father; and he wept some for the poor dead sheep, he couldn't help it. But by the time they stumbled through the woods into the welcome Hawley pasture, Benjamin Brant had no more tears, only a fist knotted below his throat, inside this time and paining some, a fist of anger he could not swallow.

Once in their loft and nestled on their beds, Melly slept within moments; but Benjy lay wide awake, excitement prickling under his clenched fingers and behind his squeezed-together eyelids.

CHAPTER THREE

Benjy Stands Against His Father

MORNING came too soon. Knowing all he now knew, Benjy could have waited a long time for that dawn. But it came on time, fresh and pale; and with it, no longer the smoke but the crisp dewy smell of new hay from the field Hawley had cut, and the slight musk odor of the sheep who were in the near pasture. The sight and sound of the sheep themselves, added to the pervasive smell of their presence, when Mistress Brant opened the cabin door to the bright day, made Benjy a little sick with remembrance. Nobody could kill their sheep as he had seen Congers' . . . nobody could. He wanted to go butt his head into his father's stomach as he had done sometimes when he was much younger, crying out, "No, no, Paw! don't let them do it!" But, of course, he couldn't tell about their excursion. It was bad, too, about the gun. If his father asked, he would have to tell, especially at a family crisis like that. He felt for the horrid sixpence in his pocket.

After a long while he was able to bring himself to look at the coin. Quite an ordinary sixpence it was, with a picture of the king on it. Benjy hid it under his mattress of corn husks on the corner plank of his bed. But then an hour later he went back and got it and put it in his pocket again as a token against foolhardiness in the future. After all, he needn't have panicked and run down the hill like that; he had looked on death before as any pioneer boy had. He had hunted and killed himself, but for reason: for food and against depredation, not wantonly. The fist was still in his chest, almost token enough without the sixpence piece.

He pumped water for the sheep trough and loosed Moomoo into the field. Then he went to breakfast on yesterday's leftover johnnycake soaked in hot bacon drippings with a mug of creamy milk. Melinda was still asleep so he left the ladder against the loft edge. His father came in from the loom house before Benjy had sopped up the last of the johnnycake. He didn't seem to notice that the little girl was abed so late.

"I've left the yarn looking natural, there's no use to hide things as though we expected them," Will Brant said.

His wife turned with the milk pitcher. The color left her face and it was as white as the liquid she poured at this first word about the coming crisis. Benjy wanted to shout out, "No use indeed!" thinking of the young Bennings. But every time he wanted to speak out, he knew he must not.

After a long sigh of resolution, Mistress Brant asked, "Will, shall you stand about all the day and do nothing?"

"What's to do, woman, tell me. What's to do?"

"Something, anything . . ."

"We can't hide ninety sheep, Anna-Mary, wi' ewes lambing to boot. Big Bertha had twins last night," Will Brant said.

Benjy blundered into the conversation, loudly but not wisely. "We could hide Moomoo and your firearms!" His father looked at him with a show of interest. "I could take Moomoo deep in the woods where 'twould be too much trouble for them to look."

Anna-Mary looked from the boy to her husband.

"Aye," Will approved calmly. "That's an all right sort

of idea. You can take your own gun and two of mine wi'
you. When they begin to come, Benjy, the soldiers . . .
about four o'clock they should be to Todd's, I reckon, and
we'll hear the ruckus."

Benjy bent over his plate as his face reddened at mention
of his gun.

"We could hide some of the new bolts of cloth, maybe,"
Anna-Mary suggested, "but where?"

"You could take 'em to Hawley's," Benjy proposed.

"No." That was all his father said, just the negative hard.
Mistress Brant's hands shook so that she set the pitcher
down. "Maybe under the mattresses?" she asked next,
timidly.

"First place they'd look!"

"But if they didn't find any," Benjy said, "couldn't ye
nail some up under the runners of the trundle bed with a
piece of old canvas?"

His father almost smiled as he nodded. "Aye, that might
be worth trying. If they tear up the big bed and find nothing, they might not expect anything to be under the trundle bed. Bring the best bolts upstairs, Anna-Mary, and I'll
hunt a piece of old canvas. Benjy, you can run to Hawleys'
and borrow some nails. I'm not against borrowing nails;
you needn't say for what!"

"Yes, Paw." He was up from table and out like a bolt,
but then the lambs with their fleece curling under the
bright morning sunshine gave him pause and he swallowed
hard.

Coming back afterward with the nails, he asked,
"Couldn't we hide the lambs in the woods, too, Paw?"

"And have them suspect a flock wi' none? And search
the woods and kill Moomoo, too, and burn our house for
very spite?"

28

"Why can't you lie a little white lie, Paw? Tell 'em we're Tory and gi' 'em their pick of the bolts to carry off. Why, huh?" Benjy asked suddenly. He could see his father's anger cross his face like a gray shadow; it was still, cold anger.

"Hawley tell you that, boy?"

"No, Paw, not this morning!"

"Hear me, I don't lie to save my neck . . . or my sheep . . . or my home even! Don't you understand? It's like believin' in God somewhat." It might have been better if he had shouted but he was quiet.

Anna-Mary turned from kneading dough and looked from her son to her husband. Benjy's feelings worked up into his face. He licked his lips. Finally he said, "Can't you just say nothin', Paw? Just keep quiet?"

"I can try that but they want an oath of allegiance; sometimes they want it in writing if a man can write and I can enough!"

"I don't understand," Benjy whispered; and he meant he could not understand why his father was making such an issue of signing his name to a document that might be lost in a soldier's knapsack. It never occurred to the boy that the paper might survive to stand for or against them in another political climate. And he did not recognize at all that his father was talking about his inner feelings and convictions.

"No matter," Will Brant said. "Help your mother bring in the best bolts to hide."

The boy didn't move at all; he just stood there. His feet were spread a little apart and his hands were rolled into fists. Eventually, he blurted out, "You mean to tell me that you'd die with the sheep first than to say a silly thing about working for King George? Would you, would you do that, Paw?" His face grew pinched and dark; he rubbed at his left eye with one fist. Then he whispered, "I went down to Congers' last night and I *saw it* . . . Will you let it happen so to us, Paw? To my ewe Bettina who's to lamb any minute?"

His father scarcely seemed to notice what he said, that he'd been down to Congers' in the middle of the night, a thing that should have got him thrashed.

"A man can die, Benjy, with a good conscience and live with a bad one, some day you'll understand all this."

"No, I'll not, never, never, never!" He expected his father to lunge at him for such defiance; but again Will Brant just stood. To Benjy it didn't seem especially brave, just foolish. The boy ran outside beating his fists on the knot in his chest and not relieving it.

He scoured the flock for his favorite ewe, a huge sweet-faced sheep that he had two years ago named his Bettina. She was heavy with the lamb she carried, but she nuzzled him affectionately and munched the bunch of sweet clover he picked at the fieldstone fence line. He gave her a hug, furtively, as though he felt he was too big for that sort of nonsense.

Melinda woke up when they began hammering the nails into the canvas on the other side of the loft partition. They had put four bolts of good wool against the slats of the trundle bed and then the canvas. It was enough wool to see them through the winter perhaps; but if the sheep were killed and the loom house destroyed, what would come of the spring? Benjy tried not to think of that. After lunch, Will Brant put his oldest gun up on the hooks over the hearth and put the two good ones behind the cabin door with a canvas knapsack of bullets he had just recently molded. The afternoon dragged.

Along about five o'clock, the sound of a single horseman startled everyone. A British soldier came cantering up to the cabin door at full speed. "Holloa!" he shouted. Almost as though he had brought it with him, the smell of smoke wafted over the woods afresh, as it had done the day before.

Will Brant filled his own doorway; he was a big man, broad-shouldered; he shook his thick curly hair back and set his hands akimbo in full sight.

"I'm to take preliminary oaths of allegiance. Are you for King George, Mister? Are you for the king?"

"We have no king in Caroline," Will Brant stated quietly.

The soldier did not rile. But he had a horse pistol in his right hand, and it looked a mean weapon for all Benjy had heard that horse pistols were inaccurate and hard to handle. The range was short enough. Melinda ran whimpering behind her mother's skirts on the other side of the table.

"Hush, don't cry," Mistress Brant said.

"We're riding the country round, likely you've heard?" the soldier said.

Mr. Brant nodded.

"I'm wi' Major Wemyss and we're punishing them as does not take the oath. You've two hours to think about it."

"I have that?" Will Brant inquired with a certain bold insolence in his tone.

"I'd mind my tongue and manners," the soldier admonished. "And be not armed when we come or we'll be killin' more than your stock, sirrah."

"I be not armed," said Benjy's father, opening his big hands with the same near insolence that pricked his son with fear and pride mixed.

The soldier pulled his rein and turned his horse and

rode across their front pasture. He leaped the stile at a good run. On the other side he waved the pistol and fired it in the air making a terrible blast. Melinda screamed.

Benjy tugged at his father's upper arm. "Paw! Paw, for God's sake, sign the oath. 'Tis a small thing," he cried. "Hold your tongue and sign it, and tomorrow we can believe what we will."

"Are you my son?" his father roared. "And know you not what an oath is? A bond, a trust before and under the God you just called upon . . . are you a coward, boy?"

"I don't know," the boy said honestly. "But I would not be a brave fool."

Behind him, his mother burst into tears. Will Brant stepped back from the doorway. Benjy ran out past him. He tore across the kitchen garden and into the sheepfold barn and up the notched footway. He threw himself on his back into a pile of hay and lay kicking his heels futilely. It was there that Alice Hawley found him a while later.

CHAPTER FOUR

A Plan for Bettina

ALICE came and sat on the mound of hay, too. She began picking at the straws, idly, bending them into pleats.

"Melly told me you went down to Congers' last night?" she began.

Benjy nodded. "It was horrible, it made me sick at my stomach, and I don't get that way easy."

Alice scratched a mosquito bite under her stocking in the middle of her leg. She was a pretty little girl except for her freckles; and Benjy rather liked those, too. And he liked her mostly because she was sensible and not silly and giggly like many girls.

"Don't you come outside and look, Alice, if . . . if they do ours like they did Congers', ye hear?"

"They needn't, that's just it," Alice cried. "Paw says, my paw says that your paw could declare he's for King George and that'd be all there was to't . . ."

"He won't," Benjy answered darkly.

"Why? His name isn't on any militia list or anything, is it?"

Benjy shrugged. "I don't think. But then it might be; he was fightin' in Savannah last year, you know. But he stands for the colony, and he won't take a false oath even though 'tis a burnin', slaughterin' soldier he takes it to. I don't understand it, Alice," he gulped hard. "My . . . my Bettina's to lamb any time now. She was sunken before the hips this

33

mornin' and it could be any minute, poor old thing!"

"That's awful, Benjy. Can't you hide her?"

"No, but I am to take Moomoo into the woods deep, just before dusk. You can smell the smoke all over again, can't you? They must be burnin' somebody else's place." They both sniffed uncomfortably.

Alice continued picking at the straws. Suddenly she said, "Benjy, maybe you could put Bettina in our flock, do you think?"

"Don't you count nights?"

"Not always, lots of times we don't; and with the excitement of the soldiers coming, nobody'd know but us."

Benjy thought for a while. Both children were exceptionally quiet. Outside someone was pumping water. They could hear it splashing into the bucket. Finally, Benjy spoke, "If they don't get here too fast, before I can hide Moomoo and get back . . . I'm not to come back, you know, and 'tis just as good because one of those British officers knows what I look like . . ." He started then to tell her the whole story of the night before. He realized that it was better to tell someone; talking to Alice eased the knot in his chest quite a bit. He concluded, "So you see, I'm supposed to stay in the woods with Moomoo until after the soldiers go. I'm to take our best guns, too; I wish I'd not lost mine. But I'm thinking that maybe I could tie Moomoo, if I can find a good spot where she wouldn't be too pinched by trees to move around. I hope she doesn't bellow. Maybe I can get Paw to let me take Melly and she can stay with Moomoo?"

But Alice shook her head. Benjy knew, too, that Melinda would be too scared to stay alone.

"Well, thank you for thinking of it, and I'll try, Alice, I'll try to sneak in without anybody seeing and slip Bettina into your flock until morning. Then we'd have her . . . and her baby when it comes . . . if . . . if they murder all ours, that's what it is, just plain ugly murderin' of innocent beasts!" He turned into the straw and hid his face.

Alice thought he might cry and she didn't want to be there. "I'll wish on it on first star I see tonight," she whispered and ran off.

Dusk thickened to darkness. Everything seemed so normal, as if they shouldn't be all keyed up waiting for something to happen. Even supper was natural enough and tasted good. Afterward Benjy milked Moomoo as usual. The only thing he didn't do was put the milk in the spring house. Instead he walked up over their two back hills to the far creek and set the bucket in a shallow place among the ferns and arrowheads. By the time Benjy got back, his father had decided the time had come to take Moomoo and the guns to the woods. Benjy asked about Melly.

"No, indeed, she's to stay right here in the house and go to bed at moonrise, oath-taking soldiers or not," his mother said.

So in the first sweet cool of the evening, Benjy slung the rifles over his shoulder, the bullet sack across his back. Pulling Moomoo on a short halter, he went well into the thick of the woods and searched a few familiar copses where the trees widened out into small glens. Finally, he found one he liked. Moomoo was in a good mood; she found some tender fern leaves to nibble and seemed happy to fend for herself. He looped her halter around a stout tree. Then he hid the rifles and the bullet sack carefully under leaves. Anyone finding Moomoo would still not discover the firearms at all, he felt certain.

Thinking of Bettina, Benjy hurried back. Cautiously, he loped out of the woods about a half mile down from their front pasture and went around the back circuitously. All seemed quiet, though he thought he had heard rowdy noise and yelling through the woods, coming from McGarve's.

The sheep were between their two hills; one hill had been wooded and not all the tree stumps had been removed. Will Brant seldom grazed the sheep there but this night he must have thought to put them some distance from the cabin.

Benjy went among the flock, thumping this one and that, stopping to stroke the flat head of a favorite, listening for the familiar bell of the old ram, the bellwether. The lambs seemed quieter than usual, not so playful even though it was glistening moonlight already, everywhere. Bettina came to Benjy. She mewed and wrinkled up her lips and pushed her flat teeth against his hand. But she didn't seem to want to follow him when he coaxed.

Benjy realized that she must be very close to her time. Would she really lamb that night? In all this furor of trouble? He simply had to get her to safety. He put his arm around her neck and walked stooped with her, coaxing, whispering endearments as he used to do when she was just a young ewe and he had chosen her for his very own. Step by step, he got her down the hill on a long diagonal toward the Hawley line. He would have to take her quite a roundabout way through a small break in the Hawley's fieldstone wall. This would take precious time. A couple of younger ewes nosed around, and Benjy had to keep sending them back when he finally got Bettina separated from the flock. Sheep are notoriously nosey, always poking their flat faces where they oughtn't! And twice Bettina just stopped and wouldn't budge. Benjy was almost at his wits' end. And to make things worse, he hadn't even gotten out of their north field and into Hawley's when he heard the noisy arrival of the soldiery: clanking of spurs and swords, a couple of pistol shots, shouting and yelling.

How long could his father hold the troopers from their vengeance, punishment as they had called it? And would he try at all? Or would he be so defiant that they would fire his very cabin over his head? And was Moomoo all right in the woods? Would she hear echoes of the noise and get excited and try to get loose? All these questions tormented the boy.

"Bettina, come, come," he coaxed. "You must get on with it." He couldn't see Hawley's flock anywhere either, not in any of their back pastures. He scanned the moonlit darkness and kept an ear on the shouting of the soldiers at his father's place. He couldn't make out much. But the soldiers had torches that flickered and flashed around the cabin, making everything look eerie. Finally cresting a small hill, Benjy came upon the Hawley sheep being brought in by one of the hired shepherds. This now posed a new problem for Benjy. He'd have to get Bettina down by the sheepfold before the young man got all the Hawley sheep penned in.

Pushing and prodding, Benjy shoved Bettina down the slope and across the meadow, taking care that she stepped cautiously on her spindly legs. Lonely now in her obvious separation from her flock, Bettina cooperated better as though anxious to get back with her own kind. The last hundred yards she would have to go alone or the hireling shepherd would notice Benjy escorting her and suspect something. If only he wasn't counting the flock; he didn't seem to be. He was calling the sheep in and poking with his stick. He noticed Bettina as soon as Benjy crouched down and let her go on alone.

"Hey, Nannie-ho!" the shepherd called, recognizing her

unwieldy shape, "get along in here, Mother, for the night . . ."

Within moments, Bettina was safely housed and the gate swung shut and latched. The young herdsman went his way up to the Hawley house. Benjy waited a safe while, listening for sound from over the hill at his home. At length, some animal shrieked and then another. A flare of bright flame licked above the hill crest, their loom house it must be! So his father had been defiant enough.

Horsemen came in sight along Hawley's dirt road, turned around and went back. Frightened, Benjy almost turned to run; then he remembered what had happened the last time he had been so foolish. He was closer to the Hawley sheepfold than to anything else safe. He scrambled down to it as soon as the last horse had been turned. He climbed the gate without even trying to unlatch and re-latch it. Inside, among the sheep he felt secure. As his heart began to beat more normally, he looked for Bettina. She had found herself a lambing stall and was mewing loudly. She was about to give birth, Benjy was sure. Well, she had never had any trouble . . . he stayed away putting himself between her and the lumbering flock who were shoving each other at the salt licks and the long feed trough.

In half an hour Bettina had dropped her first lamb and was licking it clean. Benjy knew quickly that she was going to have twins. Just then he heard a commotion outside and almost in a panic, he realized that the soldiers had arrived at Hawley's. Where to hide? Suppose they came in and counted the sheep?

Benjy found a narrow cubbyhole between the last lambing stall and the far wall of the fold. Here he crouched down as low as he could get and then he prayed fervently. It was smelly, and the atmosphere was thick in the low shed. The restless sheep constantly moved about. Nearby

Bettina kept mewing and moaning. Benjy longed to know if the second lamb had been born alive and all right.

In a moment or two, the outside commotion became more defined; then a lantern flickered against the far wall and on the ceiling. The gate was drawn out.

Someone asked, "How many sheep do you own?"

"How many sheep do I own?" Aaron Hawley repeated the question, almost as though he was stalling for time as he came quite into the fold.

"You know, don't you?" the British officer asked sharply. "Or be ye not as loyal as you claim and housing your neighbor's for hire, eh?"

Benjy almost gasped. They knew all the tricks, these soldiers; and what would Aaron Hawley say? Surely he knew how many sheep he had had that day, or could he also have expected new lambs? Had the hireling youth counted after all?

He must have because the next thing Aaron Hawley said was, "My shepherd counted as he let them out this morning and there were one hundred fifty-seven."

"Run them out past me and Bobby here will count," the officer said harshly with the implication that "you'd better be right or else."

"You may find some new lambs, I had several ewes ready," Alice's father mentioned casually.

Benjy chewed his cheeks, frightened. Did the one hundred fifty-seven include Bettina? Of course not. The next ten minutes dragged. Finally the soldier who was counting, the officer, and Mr. Hawley all came close to Benjy's hiding place and discovered Bettina.

"Well, indeed, you do have an addition to your flock and what an addition!" exclaimed the officer. "Does this happen often?"

Bettina must have had her second lamb; Benjy's heart

leaped for joy as he snuggled as tightly as possible in his nook.

"Frequently enough," Mr. Hawley replied. Then they all went out.

When he was sure it was safe, Benjy straightened up and went around to look at Bettina. She had not had *two* lambs, but *three*. His very own ewe had favored him with triplets! He was so proud that he hugged Bettina right there, kneeling on the dirt floor. Then he touched the still-sticky little lambs gingerly, just a love-pat or two apiece because much as she knew and loved and trusted him, Bettina was chary of her small fry. It was safe now, Benjy supposed, to go off and leave the ewe with the flock that was at liberty to go in or out since Mr. Hawley had left the gate open. The boy went out reluctantly though. Directly before him, he could see the blazing loom house that had taken his father so many painstaking work hours to build and equip. Benjy choked and ran among the shadows down the Hawley pasture to the woods, back to Moomoo and his trust.

He never once looked behind him again, fearing what else he might see.

CHAPTER FIVE

A Fresh Start

BENJY found Moomoo contented enough. She was chewing her cud patiently and welcomed him with a low moo. He made himself comfortable with his back against a birch tree. It was a bit damp and chilly; September usually ran swiftly into fall. The smell of smoke was thick; it seemed more intimate and meaningful because Benjy knew it was from their loom house. He just had to keep switching his thoughts to Bettina and the three beautiful babies in Hawley's shed. Eventually the tired boy dozed off, his head dropping upon his chest.

A clomping of heavy boots startled him awake. He did not know what to do. Was he discovered? It was too late to get one of the guns. Besides, his father had told him not to load them, not to make any resistance.

"Benjy?" The voice came cautious but familiar; it was his father's.

"Yes, Paw, we're here safe." Benjy sprang up.

"Come on home wi' me then. 'Tis finished. I reckon we can douse the fire more though. Aaron Hawley's come down to help pump and carry."

"They burned us then?" Benjy asked, reluctant to admit that he already knew a great deal.

"Aye." His father said.

They went back through the woods single file. Will

41

Brant carried the guns, and Benjy took the bullet sack and Moomoo's halter.

As they broke out of the tree line, Mr. Brant said, "I've butchered eight of the sheep. I reckon that's all we can keep. You'll have to help me bury the rest tomorrow. Tie Moomoo outside the shed."

Benjy looked at his father in the moonlight; the round pumpkin moon was just sinking. "Did they kill all our sheep, did they? Did they, Paw?" All the Hawleys and his mother and Melinda were making a bucket brigade from the well and the trough pump to the smoldering ruin of the loom house. It seemed like a bad dream.

"Aye, they killed our sheep; but they didn't find the wool we hid and they left me the old gun because they couldn't find any others," Mr. Brant said.

"Hear me, Paw, I hate your letting them kill our sheep, when you might've spoke to save them, y'hear! I hate your letting them do't," Benjy blazed out. He was astonished at his own boldness.

His father just set the two long rifles against the cabin wall and reached for the buckets he had set down when he went off to the woods. He handed one to his son. He never said another thing about what had happened that night.

Melinda told Benjy how the soldiers had come tramping their horses right through the kitchen garden, asking Will Brant for his oath. He had stepped back into his cabin and bade them search it for what they wanted. He said he had no guns but the old one over the 'place and no wool but the unloomed in the loom house. They had romped all over, opened cupboards, poked in the chests; they had torn up Melly's bed and Benjy's; they had stuck their curved sabers through the mattress of Will's and Anna-Mary's bed while everyone stood by, holding their breath. But then they had not looked in the trundle bed, just shoved it part out and poked beneath the big bed at it.

Yet moments later, when Will Brant refused to speak for the king or to sign a loyalty statement, they fired the loom house directly. Then a half dozen went out and killed the sheep.

"They hollered, the sheep, some of 'em; it was awful, jest awful!" Melly reported; she'd heard some of it but she hadn't seen it, for her mother had kept her inside and hid her head under an apron.

"Paw needn't have, he needn't," Benjy began, his fists knotted; but then he realized it was over; getting upset wouldn't help.

With no further protest, as dawn broke, the boy went to work with his father burying the sheep. It took most of the day. He couldn't go to Bettina and he really didn't know what to do about her either; suppose Mr. Hawley thought she was part and parcel of his flock now?

With the Hawleys' help, the Brants had been able to get the loom house fire under control and out fairly fast. Fortunately, too, the soldiers had not elected to stay in the neighborhood as they had at Congers'. They had left immediately after looking at Hawley's sheep.

In late afternoon, when the loom house had cooled off enough, everyone went to view the damage. The building was ruined and could not be rebuilt till spring. But inside, only the corner where the unwoven wool had been was completely charred. Parts of the great loom could be repaired, a winter's work, but something Mr. Brant could do since no sheep were left to shear, no wool to card and spindle into thread and weave. Of course, the Brants had no savings to buy a new flock; Benjy thought about that as he swept out debris and scraped away burnt areas from the loom framework. He wanted to get Bettina and her babies. Surely, they would be able to walk from the Hawley fold now. The boy grew more and more impatient. Finally, he walked right up to his father and said, "Paw, excuse me a bit, I'll be right back."

This was the first thing he had said to his father. Mr. Brant nodded his head and the boy ran off, down to the stile and over and up to Hawley's. As he went, Benjy wasn't sure what he would do. Just coax Bettina after him, he supposed; she was his, nobody could deny that.

However, when Benjy reached the pen, the hireling shepherd was there cutting out snarls on a couple of fat ewes. Bettina was standing nearby nursing one triplet and keeping a motherly eye on the other two. Benjy slowed down, stopped, spoke a polite "Goodday." He couldn't think of anything else to say when the fellow nodded cheerily. Bettina baaed; just possibly she recognized Benjy. He almost put out a hand to her.

"Did ye come to get that big flock of yours back home?" a burly voice broke in. Aaron Hawley came out of the shed laughing, with Alice behind him.

Benjy looked up at him shyly. "So you knew?" he asked.

"Last night when the lieutenant came to count? Yea, I knew; and I saw ye hiding, too, but they didn't. Reckon I could've got me a kissin' cousin quick enough though if they had."

Benjy didn't tell Mr. Hawley a word about the other officer that had threatened to remember how he looked. He thanked both Alice and her father for their kindness. Then Alice helped him guide Bettina and the lambs home to stand outside the loom house.

"Paw," Benjy called. His father came out. How odd he looked, hot, sweaty and covered with soot. "Paw," Benjy announced, "I've brought Bettina; she's alive with three lambkins. We can start our flock afresh," he said proudly.

Will Brant knelt down in the grass. "God bless," was all he said. It was enough.

After supper, Benjy told the whole story of how he had managed Bettina's escape. Later, Aaron Hawley came down and offered a young ram and several yearling ewes to start a new flock for the Brants, if Will would set out his kitchen garden for him the next spring. Aaron claimed he was not good with vegetables; quickly, they had a bargain, and everyone laughed. Anna-Mary made chocolate and warmed up some leftover gingerbread. Benjy began to forget the trench between their hills where they had buried the sheep.

CHAPTER SIX

Conflict Comes Closer

SEPTEMBER's weather continued bright and warm until the last ten days. Brisk breezy nights ripened apples and pumpkins, dried corn, grew thick fleece on the sheep. But then toward the end of the month it rained and rained, until the children thought it would never stop.

The rain slinked and slithered along the roof slabs and slopped into the fieldstone troughs Benjy's father had just finished making that very summer. Melinda, standing on a great chest beneath their only window, listened to the splatter of the drops on the greenish glass bottles and traced the faint rivulets of descending water with her forefinger. Candles were lit on the big plank table. Scarcely any light at all penetrated through the bottles from the gray stormy day.

"I wish 'twould stop, just rain, rain, rain," Melly grumbled.

"Oh, 'tain't been rainin' that long," her brother said.

"Two whole days and Paw gone and you without enough wood cut to last beyond tomorrow."

"Lawdy, you're as crotchety as an old woman already and you not yet nine," Benjy protested.

"I'll play you draughts and betcha my piece of gingerbread at supper I win," Melinda suggested, scrambling up their ladder for their homemade game box.

"Lie down, Striker," Benjy ordered the dog who had risen from before the hearth with a low growl. Striker did not lie down at the command. Instead his fur bristled and he barked. "No draughts, Melly, hush up, somebody's comin'," Benjy called up.

Melly started down the ladder. "Paw?" she asked.

"Don't reckon; Striker'd not bark at Paw." Benjy slid the peek-panel on their thick door. " 'Tis two men on horses and Paw walked, remember?"

Melinda came to set her face beside her brother's. She had to strain on tiptoe to see out. The horsemen faded in and out of view as gusts of wind swept the heavy rain across the children's line of vision. But as the strangers came within sound, their horses sloshing in the mud, they could be recognized as frontiersmen, coarsely clothed, skin-capped. The dog began barking in earnest. Benjy slammed the peep-shutter closed. Mistress Brant came down from her attic bedroom. The roll of a heavy fist rattled upon the cabin door.

"Will home?" a big voice asked. Benjy thought it sounded like John Sevier.

"Went huntin' afore this storm and hasn't got back yet; he might have holed up somewhere," Mistress Brant opened the door in. Striker, at her side, began wagging his tail, recognizing one of the men, too. "You'll be wantin' some supper? We've chickens."

"Wouldn't go bad; 'tis about that time and no weather for goin' on," the second man said, rubbing his belly.

"Thank ye kindly," the first man added. Benjy saw that it was John Sevier.

"Come on in and sit down at table," Mistress Brant gestured; then she raised her voice and called, "Melly!"

The little girl came skipping with a "Yes, Maw."

"Set that pan o' pone in the oven, girl, and turn the birds on the spit reg'lar now, they're most done. I wish your Paw would get home. *Benjy?*"

He had hung back waiting for that inevitable call. He scuttled before the visitors with a polite "Evening," his curly brown head lowered.

"You go put the horses in our shed, 'tis no weather for critters to be out in when we got shelter," his mother observed.

The boy hustled. He didn't want to miss the men talking about why they had come. As he came back into the welcome warmth and dryness of their big cabin, he heard Sevier saying, " . . . well, this Scotsman's goin' about settin' afore folks' fires and cajolin' 'em into signing loyalty oaths . . ."

Mistress Brant wiped her hands on her apron and began putting out big scoured wooden trenchers. "He's not been settin' in my kitchen," she laughed. "I heard though from the tin peddler last week. But we had our chance at signin' loyalty oaths last month when that Major Wemyss burned our loom house and killed our sheep. Besides, my brother was massacred at the Waxhaws and so was Will's cousin!"

Benjy knew she meant that terrible day the past May when dozens of their friends and relatives had been killed after they had laid down their arms and called for "Quarter."

"We've need of every fellow we can round up to wipe out this character before he succeeds in his mission. He's pleasanter than most Britishers. We're all to meet at the Watauga Flats next Tuesday night and we'll be wantin' Will there," Sevier said next.

Mistress Brant set out the chickens on a wooden platter and cut them in half. Benjy laid a piece in each trencher. Melinda handed around baked yams and tender, hot, buttered cornbread. Everyone fell to and ate heartily, including the two children who sat mute, as good children ought, at the end of the table.

Afterward, the two men drank hot cider sitting before the great fireplace until Sevier insisted that they had better be on their way. Benjy found a scarf to wrap about his head in preparation for ducking out through the downpour to get the visitors' horses.

"Don't forget to tell your old man our message, Mistress Brant," the broad-shouldered Sevier cried, picking up his knapsack and rifle.

"Tell me what?" roared a loud voice as the door swung in on its thick leather hinges.

Will Brant was soaked clear through to his skin, but he had a mess of rabbits and wild turkeys slung on his back. He pulled off his stocking cap and laid his burden on the wide hearthstone where it promptly created a puddle. Sevier slapped him a friendly greeting across the shoulders and sent a spray of water in every direction. Melinda giggled.

"No laughin' matter this storm," her father chided, pinching her fat rosy cheek. "However, I had pretty good hunting and I holed up in a cave I know for a while. But since it didn't stop, I decided to head home anyway. What's to do, boys?"

"We're aimin' to lick this fellow Ferguson that's roustin' about for the king . . . to meet at Watauga Flats Tuesday night and corner him somewhere about the Mountain thereafter. Suit you right, Will?" Sevier asked.

"You bet I'll be there."

Benjy pulled at the wet fringe of his father's linsey-woolsey hunting shirt. "Take me, too, Paw. Can I go?" he begged.

" 'Tis for grown men, Benjy, no larkin' business. We'll

be aimin' to shoot them British and Scots for keeps."

"Like they did to Uncle Toby?" Melinda put in quickly, and her mother hurried a hand across her mouth.

But John Sevier laughed. "Yea, Melly, for keeps like they killed your poor uncle. No quarter like he got and the password's to be Buford, I hear, and 'twas Colonel Buford's massacred command your uncle got killed in, huh?"

Melly knew and nodded.

"Password to be Buford? That rides all right with me," Will Brant said. "I'll be there, you can count. Go along, Benjy boy, get the men their horses."

"That's all he ever lets me do," Benjy pouted to Melinda as he went out. "Go git the horses, that's all. When'll I be big enough to do more? I can shoot game good enough when he takes me along." This was true; he was good with his rifle, could bark a squirrel as neatly as any man, striking near enough to kill the animal by concussion without marking it. In fact, Benjy was so good with a gun that his mother had sent to her sister-in-law's for the dead uncle's Kentucky to replace the Dekkard Benjy had finally confessed losing at Congers'.

"Hush up, boy," his father said, recognizing his murmur of protest. "Time's coming when you'll be man enough to make you sick of't, believe me." And Benjy thought of that night he had gone out with Melly, alone.

It continued raining. Will Brant dressed his game and hung it up outside of his small smokehouse. He had shot a deer, too, that he'd have to fetch home on horseback as soon as it cleared, which it did at mid-morning the next day.

They found the deer as Mr. Brant had left it, gutted and hung upon a sturdy larch limb. After they got it home, it took all afternoon to skin and quarter it and put it up properly to cure. Will Brant could take off a hide as neatly as any Indian. Melinda was to have a little skirt and vest of this one, if it tanned well. She wouldn't watch the butchering, though.

Her mother scolded her. "Might not be ladylike to know such things, but where we be, you'd better learn all you can for survivin', girl."

Mistress Brant worried a good bit. She remembered too well earlier Indian troubles. Thus the plans for the next Tuesday troubled her though she could say nothing against her husband's going. She remembered, too, as did Benjy, that she had argued with him about his stubbornness in the matter of the loyalty oath. If he would go, he would. Frontier folk rarely thought of joining the Continental army as regular soldiers, but when the fighting came close to home, as had the massacre at the Waxhaws and Wemyss and the sheep, they were afire for swift reprisal. The old justice of an eye for an eye appealed on the frontier where a man scraped and scratched and fought for every moment's peace and provision.

As he had taken pains to set things in order and to remain calm during the Wemyss incident, Will Brant again endeavored to leave his homestead in good order. He greased the door hinges, fixed the chicken coop, put dry straw handy in the sheepfold where Bettina and the lambs stayed with the six yearling ewes, the ram, and one older ewe that Aaron Hawley had supplied. He mended worn spots in the tether for Moomoo and scoured their wagon and checked all harness and saddles. He sent Benjy and Melinda to sort and store ripe apples for winter eating and to string long lines of others on the drying shelf over the fireplace. The whole family went nutting every afternoon to add to the winter supply before the squirrels beat them to it.

"You'd think you were aiming to be gone a long time," Benjy remarked once.

His father looked keenly at him. "I'm not aimin' to be gone long at all, two or three days maybe, boy, but one never knows. A man can go off on something like this, and there'll be some as don't come back, mind you, and others comin' back as they'd not want to, understand?"

Benjy pushed back his thick, cropped hair. "I didn't think on that part of it," he admitted.

"Don't, son, don't think on it, but let's be prepared!" his father pulled one of his ears playfully.

"Yes, Paw."

He ran more willingly to his chores for a while. Only the last minute, when his father had saddled and bridled the wiry brown mare, checked his long rifle, tied on his bag of bullets, and filled his powder horn, did Benjy say once more wistfully, "I wish I could be goin' wi' ye."

Will Brant shook his head, wagging his coonskin cap tail. "No, boy, you stay to home and look after your maw; that's where you belong on this. I'm the man of this family and 'tis my duty to be about this business, see?"

The boy nodded, thrusting his hands deep in his trousers pockets. His father kissed his mother and Melly; then he rubbed Benjy's hair with a firm hand. "Be good and do what your maw says, no matter what," he ordered and set foot to stirrup.

"Will, don't you take chances and get you on back home here after 'tis done," Mistress Brant cried, her hands on her hips.

"I'll do that, Maw!" Will Brant cried; he tickled the horse in the ribs and she loped.

Mistress Brant darned socks that night and was very quiet. It made the children uncomfortable, her being so quiet. Benjy mentioned popping corn, but since his mother didn't respond at all, he played draughts in a corner with Melinda and made no disturbance.

The next day his mother was even quieter and more pre-occupied. Benjy supposed she knew more about the seri-ousness of the business than his father had mentioned in front of the children. The third day, everyone was glum. The Hawleys sent down to make inquiry. And the nearest patriot neighbors, the Thomsons, came over in the after-noon to see if the Brants had any news. They hadn't. The Thomson men had gone on the expedition, too.

"You reckon 'tis over, Benjy?" Tad Thomson, a boy about Benjy's age, asked.

"Yea, I reckon 'tis; they wasn't about to be putting it off. Wish Paw'd come back . . ."

"Wish mine would, too . . ."

Alice Hawley thrust in a dark thought. "Suppose the British won?"

"Aw, don't brag on your redcoats," Tad said; but Alice's question sobered both boys.

Benjy never quarreled with Alice about their differences in politics; he liked her too well for that. The Thomsons—mother, two younger sons, and baby daughter—went home at dusk. By supper, and after supper, and even by Melinda's bedtime, Will Brant had not returned. Melly wasn't asleep when Benjy came up with his stub of candle and pulled off his outer clothes and crawled into bed.

"Benjy, I been listenin' and about a half hour gone, I heard horse hoofs, as if back on Trading Road," the little girl began.

"Oh, you couldn't this far and through the walls 'n' all," Benjy poohed.

"Yes, I did hear somethin'," she insisted.

And as if in immediate corroboration, a clatter of horses sounded directly outside, followed by the pounding of a fist at their cabin door.

"What is it?" Mistress Brant called out anxiously. Benjy could picture her behind the fast bolted door, his rifle under her armpit. He didn't have to lean over the loft edge and look down at all.

"Mack Thomson, ma'am, to let you know as 'tis over wi' vict'ry, and your man be comin' soon, I reckon." The party of horsemen didn't stop but rode on across the Brants' front pasture.

Benjy's mother hurried up her narrow stair and came to where she knew his bed was on the other side of her bedroom wall. "Benjy, did you hear? Did you hear?" she called between two logs. " 'Twas win they did! Go to sleep, your father will be here soon."

The children fell asleep quickly under the pleasant relief her words had brought. The next morning, when Benjy woke and went downstairs, he saw that his mother had changed into her best dress and combed her hair prettily and gone back downstairs to wait for her husband. For she was asleep at the big table, her head on her arm. The candle had guttered out. Will Brant had not come home.

As the bright October day dawned clear, a high wind touched the tree tops and tossed multi-colored small leaves about as though it had them to burn. The two young Brants were restless as fleas and kept running as close to the Trading Road as they dared. Twice they caught glimpses of horsemen riding hard to their homes, but not their father. Late afternoon the sun went down bright russet, tinting their cornstalks orange, and still nothing. Benjy set out a new block of salt for Moomoo and finished the milking his mother had begun. Then he brought in three armloads of wood. He was on his way back to the pile he had been chopping at when a voice hailed him, a strange voice.

"Boy, this Brant's place?"

"Yes."

"Run get your maw, lad, heh? We're bringing your father home."

Benjy felt his throat lock; a chill tingled along his spine. "H-h-how?" he managed to ask, thick-tongued with his fear.

"He's hurt pretty bad, son, but he's alive," the stranger said with a backwoodsman's bluntness.

That was just the way Benjy told the news to his mother, too. She didn't cry. She caught at her shawl and ran out to where three men came in small procession, two on horses with a litter slung between and the big man who had spoken to Benjy afoot.

Benjy was never to forget how they brought his father home that day; how gingerly they carried him up the narrow stair and laid him upon his bed; how white he was; how he moaned in pain though he bit his teeth together against doing so. The men made him as comfortable as they could. As soon as they left, Mistress Brant began to poultice the ugly thigh wound. A huge trough had been made by a blast of grapeshot. Will Brant had been within too close range of one of Ferguson's twelve-pound cannon. It was a miracle his leg hadn't been blown entirely off. He had severe powder burns and the beginnings of an infection in the large wound. Mistress Brant's ministration did little good. By morning her husband was raving with fever. The two children were frightened. They had never seen anyone so sick. No glorious tale of victory did Mr. Brant tell; he just lay scratching at the bed board, trying to stifle his groans.

"Benjy, we must get a doctor. Your father can't go to one so we've to get one to come to him," Mistress Brant said that noon. "Do you think you could ride down toward Britton's? Might be a surgeon down there or somebody knowin' of one thereabouts."

Benjy knew it would be a long ride in unfamiliar country, but he felt brave enough. "I'll go, Maw," he agreed.

"Fix yourself something to eat in the knapsack and take your gun; might be marauders fixin' for vengeance or something like that. You be careful, Benjy. I need you."

"I'll be careful, Maw; do I take Bessie?"

"Yes, and roll a blanket in case you don't find adequate shelter for the night. Get out Paw's maps from the oilskin and look carefully for how to go. And make the best time you can for 'tis time that's important to your paw, I reckon. If we but had a doctor hereabout."

" 'Tain't one," Benjy said, which was certainly true. A British surgeon's mate had bound up his father's wound on the battle site. The fellow had been a prisoner; the men that brought Will Brant home had told Benjy how the young surgeon had offered his services and saved many American lives. Since his father had been saved from dying on the battlefield, Benjy recognized that the rest was up to him.

CHAPTER SEVEN

Journey in the Dark

BENJY set off eagerly yet with some fear in the pit of his stomach. He was glad to be riding Bessie, gun in holster, knapsack at his back, for all the world like a young man at last. But loneliness tautened him with every mile he left behind him. Bessie trotted fair through crunchy autumn leaves. Until it grew dark, the boy was comfortable and felt safe enough. At dusk he was skirting the edge of the Black Creek Swamp. He had been that far with his father.

The moon would rise early. Benjy checked the small map he had drawn clumsily from his father's. He knew he would not be able to look at it when it became fully dark. He figured that good luck might bring him to his destination by ten o'clock. The small brown horse kept her pace. But as the night shadows lengthened and it got colder, Benjy shivered from more than the chill. He heard few noises, however; only the yap of a young fox, the hoot of an owl, the whir of wings as the horse frightened a covey of grouse or wild turkey. Later, moonshine on the swamp water was startling, as was the shape of old stumps or the swishing of Spanish moss on the oaks that bordered the road.

For comfort, Benjy began to talk to Bessie in whispers; she pricked her ears back courteously. They rounded the swamp safely and found themselves on an even stretch down the Trading Road for a bit. Then Benjy cut across country, keeping a straight path on a diagonal. This was difficult and nerve-wracking for he could easily get off the track. He knew he was losing precious time.

Finally, Bessie rode into a little wood. Benjy hoped to go directly through it. The trees thickened, then thinned again; that was normal enough, the boy thought. He was ready to sigh with relief at the prospect of open country again, when, to his horror, a figure sprang at his bridle and caught it so hard that Bessie whinnied.

"Don't touch your gun or my man'll blast you!" a fierce voice cried, indicating the presence of more than one assailant.

Benjy froze completely. The man who had accosted him tore the reins readily from his numb fingers. Another fellow strode out of the shadows, caught at Benjy's arm and tumbled him neatly out of saddle yet standing on his feet.

"Where are you going?" this person demanded.

"To . . . to Britton's," Benjy muttered, his voice strangely feeble.

"An indirect route you're taking," the fierce voice accused.

"No, suh," the boy offered the man the courtesy his obvious authority seemed to merit. "I need a doctor . . . for my paw . . . who's hurt bad."

"Hurt bad with what? Under what circumstance?"

"I . . . uh . . . just hurt . . . bad," Benjy clammed up quickly; he knew enough not to go around bragging on fights or battles in those times.

"Bring him in," the fellow who had pulled him out of saddle commanded.

The first man who had Bessie's reins, poked a gun in Benjy's back. Prodding the boy before him, the man followed a shadowy aisle between the thinning trees. Thirty steps brought them out into a clearing where a small cabin sat, shut up and empty-looking. But upon a signal rapping, the door swung in and revealed a group of men around a stubby table.

"What have we here?" a sharp-nosed fellow with one leg raised upon a footstool demanded.

"Just a stripling boy, sir, but you said to stop anybody. He wants a doctor for his old man, says he's hurt bad," the spokesman offered.

"Where are you from, boy?" demanded the sharp-nosed man who seemed to be of considerable importance judging from the deference the others paid his every word.

"Between Cheraw and Waxhaws," Benjy answered truthfully.

"And what's it with your father? Hurt in some fighting maybe?"

Benjy didn't hesitate. "I don't know," he replied glibly. "He's just hurt bad and needs a doctor. I weren't wi' him when he done it."

One of the men at the table with his back to Benjy chuckled and muttered, "Now that's a born lawyer, that young one!"

"You had better state more, boy," the fellow with the footstool continued; he was a slight, swarthy man, with an air of distinction.

"I don't know more," Benjy insisted. The man who had laughed did so again.

A tall slender young man, well dressed in serge breeches, embroidered jacket, and ruffled neckcloth, leaned across the end of the rough table. "Hear me, boy," he said, "I'm a doctor, a surgeon, but if I'm to show an interest in your father, you'd better tell us what's the matter with him?"

Benjy remembered his father as he had left him, clawing at his bedding, his eyes burning with fever. That had been at noon that day. "If you be a doctor, come back with me at once, please," he pleaded. " 'Tis his leg . . . all torn . . . and he be out of his head with fever and pain . . . and the wound is thick with pus and sometimes bleeding. Maw has put on bread and mustard poultices but they ain't done any good."

"You Tory or Whig, boy? And was your paw hurt at King's Mountain?" the man with the fierce voice asked.

"I ain't Tory. And I told that I don't know where my paw was hurt; he weren't in no condition to tell when he come home . . . 'twas strangers who brought him. My maw ain't one to pump out a stranger," Benjy fairly shouted.

Everyone chuckled then. Benjy felt his face get hot.

"Shall I go?" the man who claimed to be a doctor asked directly of the one with the footstool.

"Why not? We can do nothing here for days. Perhaps others have need of a doctor out that way. Change your dress, 'tis not Charlestown, Hal."

"Yes, sir." The young man rose; catching another fellow by the arm, he beckoned him out with him through a rear door.

When they returned in a few minutes, the doctor was in trousers and a hunting shirt. His hair had been brushed of its powder and proved to be a dark chestnut color, tied tightly with black string. He carried a square leather case which Benjy supposed contained his medicines and instruments. "Come along, boy, and I pray you know your way for I do not," he said.

"If ye put me back where they stopped me and turn me about-face, I'll find my way," Benjy said, with more hope than confidence.

"I'll pick you up, Hal, within a week, if anything comes up for us," said the broad-shouldered fellow with the boisterous laugh. He did not turn so Benjy could not see his face but he asked, "What's your father's name, boy, so I know to ask my way?"

"Brant," Benjy admitted at last, seeing no way out of it.

"Brant? Will Brant of Cheraw? The devil take me! Why'n't you say so before?" the man asked. "Be off, Hal, and take pains to save us a good man, you hear?"

The doctor grinned. "I take pains to save 'em regardless of their religion or their politics."

So Benjy found himself released in the custody of the young surgeon who led the way back to where Bessie had been tethered.

Near dawn they reached the Brant homestead. Striker was waiting beside the pump, his tail wagging gaily. Mistress Brant ushered the young doctor to the side of her sick husband. Mr. Brant looked much worse to Benjy, gray-faced, almost unconscious, breathing heavily.

The surgeon sent both children out of the way downstairs. Benjy fell asleep on their hard settle beside the fireplace, cushioned only on the woolen jacket he had taken off. He was so tired that he did not even think of going up to his bed. But sounds from the back bedroom disturbed his sleep. Whatever the doctor did, it caused Will Brant to cry out now and then and to moan almost continuously. Benjy's rest was troubled not merely by these outcries of his father but by ugly dreams in which he seemed to be trying to ride Bessie away from some stranger who kept pulling her back by a long bridle rope.

At noon, Anna-Mary Brant woke her son. While Benjy and Melinda set the table, putting a place for the doctor, they heard their father scream twice. In a little while the doctor came downstairs and ate a hearty lunch, quite calmly. This made Benjy resentful; and the boy angered when the young man went off on his horse afterward.

"I can do no more now. I shall ride about the neighborhood and see if others need my service," the young man told Mistress Brant, with a casualness that seemed like indifference to Benjy.

"You'd think he'd finish one job before be began another," Benjy blurted out.

"Hush!" his mother cried. "He came a long way to help us, and others. He be obligated to do as wide and efficient a service as might be necessary."

"Has he helped anything with Paw?"

"I don't know," Mistress Brant admitted. " 'Tis too early to tell much."

"I don't like him," Benjy decided emphatically. His mother again told him to hush.

"I like him," Melinda put in. "He's got a kind face."

"Bah," Benjy scoffed and went out to tend to Moomoo and the chickens. He had lots to do with his father abed; he did it willingly enough most of the time.

The whole afternoon went by. The surgeon did not return, but about dusk, Will Brant woke out of his half-coma and drank some broth and soaked bread. He even took a cup of hot milk with a bit of their precious Jamaica rum in it. At dark, the doctor returned and bled his patient a little. Then he ate a hearty supper and went to bed on Benjy's bed. The boy had Melinda's and she went to sleep in the trundle bed which she had not done for three years.

Whether Benjy liked the young doctor or not, Will Brant improved under his care. By Saturday night he could sit up for a few minutes and talk.

"You reckon I'll have full use of my leg again, Doctor," he asked once.

The young man who had given his name as Haldon Wartley nodded. "I believe you will, if all goes well from now on; but it will not be soon. 'Tis a good thing your wife and the boy are handy," he observed.

Will said, "Aye," and Benjy made a face at Melinda behind the doctor's back.

Striker, lying before the fireplace, bristled suddenly, then growled. Even upstairs, everyone heard the clop-clop of a horse outside. Benjy ran down and took a gun to the door.

"Who's there?" he shouted. His mother and the surgeon came part way down and gave him courage. After-dark callers on the frontier always aroused anxiety.

"You've Dr. Hal Wartley here?" a firm voice demanded. It was a voice Benjy had heard before but he could not have immediately told where.

"Yes, suh." He opened up.

The man had to stoop to get in. He was quite the tallest fellow Benjy had ever seen, a big robust man with startling steel-blue eyes and a mane of wavy reddish hair.

"Good evening, ma'am. I've tied my horse at your trough if that's all right?"

She nodded.

"I've come to get the doctor," he continued. "What of your husband, Mistress, does he improve?"

"Yes, slowly," she said.

Dr. Wartley came to stand beside his hostess. Mistress Brant gestured the stranger into the big room that served the cabin as kitchen, dining room, living quarters.

The tall man closed the heavy door and pulled the latch string in. He quite dominated the room. Flinging back a dark blue cape, he revealed the blue and white of a North Carolinian infantry uniform with the single silver epaulet of a captain. "Mistress Brant, I know your husband from the battle at King's Mountain and I had hoped to recruit him for a band we're forming under Colonel Francis Marion. I'm Captain David Lind, at your service."

Benjy's mother half curtsied.

"I take it your husband's participation in our little enterprise must be postponed. But we're in no particular hurry; it may well be a month before we have an actual call to duty," the captain continued.

"May I offer you some supper?" Mistress Brant asked.

"It would be most welcome and I'd like to stay the night. I've rid all day," he admitted.

Benjy stood staring at him. He knew now which man he was, the one who had said he'd make a good lawyer. Benjy also realized that the wiry sharp little man with the footstool had been Colonel Marion. The boy stared so diligently at the captain that his mother had to tell him twice to see to his horse.

After supper, the captain and surgeon went upstairs together and talked with Will Brant. Benjy heard nothing of what was said. This made him cranky and he quarreled with Melinda until his mother boxed both their ears and settled them on a quilt before the fireplace. Later, Benjy took the quilt up into a corner of his parents' room and Melly went into the trundle bed again. The captain and the doctor bedded down on the children's beds. The dark quiet of the night settled into the cabin.

CHAPTER EIGHT

Benjy Sees Two Faces of War

CAPTAIN LIND got up betimes and pitched hay for the horses. Then he tethered Moomoo and brought in enough wood for the day. Benjy decided that he liked him immensely.

At noon, shucking corn for his mother, Benjy was startled by shouted commands. Looking up, he saw a long line of men approaching from Hawley's along the edge of the woods. Preceding were two mounted frontiersmen with their rifles cocked and at the ready in the cradle of their arms. Other mounted men so armed rode at intervals along the line of march. Benjy ran like mad across their stable yard into the cabin.

"Ca-ca-captain Lind!" he blustered, "there's soldiers comin', lots and lots of soldiers."

The captain smiled, undisturbed. "That, my boy, is the unlikeliest story I have heard in five years," he commented. Leisurely, he unfolded his long legs, rose from the bench where he was sitting, and went to the doorway.

Benjy would have gone out then, reassured by the captain's calm manner, and stood to watch the procession file past their property. But Captain Lind put his brawny arm across the cabin doorway.

"They're prisoners from the Mountain," he explained softly as Mistress Brant came to stand looking out, curious also, followed by the young surgeon. "Let them pass." The captain continued to bar the opening. Hatless and jacketless, standing there quietly in his white linen shirt, it would have been difficult for anyone outside to have recognized him as military.

The man who rode foremost on the right side with the cradled rifle nodded curtly toward the captain's huge form in the doorway and asked no questions. The column marched across the back of the Brant stable yard, past the well and the corncrib and up across the pasture.

After several segments of line had passed, Dr. Wartley observed in a low tone, "Some in that line could use my services."

The first marchers were ordinary regulars burdened with themselves alone. One or two of these had bandaged limbs but the majority were none the worse for the rigors of a two-day, almost foodless march. The mounted guardsmen stopped at Will Brant's well and horse trough, in pairs; they watered their beasts and hauled up a bucket of well water and drank themselves. Their prisoners looked longingly at the water but none stopped and none seemed to murmur. They bore the rugged jostling of their guards with fortitude. Perhaps they were already too exhausted to plead for mercy. They were hustled along in fours; if any hesitated, he was encouraged by the reins straps of one of the mounted American sergeants.

"Why don't they let 'em all drink? We've plenty of water," Benjy wondered.

No one made him any reply.

By then the rear of the column was approaching; here were a score or so of British officers Benjy could tell, by their uniforms. Unlike the first soldiers, these men were burdened, each of them, with two muskets unloaded; all were bloody and mudstained; none wore shoes, and the soles of their stockings had long since worn off and fallen out. Several struggled valiantly to keep up; it was plain to see that these were hurt, one way or another, perhaps seriously; more than one had a shoulder dyed a deeper rust than his scarlet uniform.

"By heaven, David! Some of those men need a surgeon if they are to survive!" Hal Wartley exclaimed.

"Don't be a fool, Hal, those guards are violent backwoodsmen. Let be, 'tis not our affair," the captain replied.

"Ain't they British prisoners? Ain't the guards our men?" Benjy asked. "Ain't they men like my paw that fought against the loyalty oath?"

"Yes," the captain answered him.

"Well, ain't they bein' just as cruel as the British that killed our sheep, ain't they?" the boy demanded next.

"The faces of war are always harsh, boy," Captain Lind told him. "War is a two-faced cur! I say, look the other way, this is no longer our affair."

" 'Tis mine!" cried the doctor. "I'm a surgeon and the wounded are always my affair."

The boy's admiration swung like a pendulum from the captain to the doctor. Just then a seriously wounded young British lieutenant pitched forward into the dust beyond the horse trough. A companion grasped his good arm and hauled him back on his feet; but they both abandoned their burdens of two muskets each. Immediately, one of the riding frontiersmen pulled in his horse and ordered them to retrieve the weapons. Both bent obediently; then the lieutenant stumbled and fell down heavily a second time. Benjy slipped out under Captain Lind's brawny arm and scooted toward the well before anyone could discourage him. Grabbing the tin dipper from the well rail, he dipped it into the bucket and carried drink to the suffering lieutenant who gulped the water greedily.

"Tory brat, eh? Lookin' to have your paw's place burned?" the guardsman shouted at him; then he kicked him in the back with the toe of his boot in the left stirrup.

"I ain't Tory but the man's sick. He's a human being like you, ain't he? I wouldn't treat a dog like that," Benjy blazed.

The man reached down to slap him and he ducked.

"Spunky young one," observed Captain Lind still from the doorway; but he had reached for his uniform jacket and was putting it on.

The whole column had now halted. Several other guardsmen rode back toward the well. Haldon Wartley came hurrying down from the cabin, his leather bag of instruments in hand.

"I'm a doctor," he announced, "and that man has a ball in his shoulder that should come out."

One of the frontiersmen raised a rifle nastily. "We ain't givin' no quarter, see," he said.

Captain Lind strode between the fellow's horse and the young doctor. "Let him look at the wounded, Tom," he said gently, "and let your column drink. 'Tis a long trek to more good water. This is the Brant place; 'twas one of your prisoners, no doubt, a surgeon's mate, who saved Will Brant's life."

The guardsman evidently knew Captain Lind, for he pulled his forelock under his coonskin cap in a half salute and grumbled, "Mornin', Captain, ef ye wuz to speak to the Colonel up yonder?"

Lind nodded and Haldon Wartley went to work, tearing off the bloody jacket and shirt of the young British officer right there in Benjy's back yard. Benjy hauled up well watér, and the prisoners were allowed to drink in pairs, all of them, and to lay down their burdensome rifles for a few moments. The march partner of the officer who had stumbled told Dr. Wartley that he knew of no doctors or surgeon's mates among the prisoner group. Benjy wondered what had happened to the man who had helped his father. They would never know.

Later, when the entire party had moved on, Captain Lind put a hand on Benjy's shoulder. "Like your father, boy, eh? Plenty of spunk when it's needed!" he commented kindly.

Benjy bulged a little with pride though he really hadn't been especially brave; he had just run out without thinking. Saving Bettina had taken more of what he would have considered genuine courage.

The captain and the surgeon left together that evening, late, just before the children went to bed. Lind's last words to Will Brant were, "I believe we've a month, at least, perhaps longer. I shall come back and see how your recovery is progressing. We'd like to have you with us, Will, if it's at all possible."

"And I'd like to come," Benjy's father said, fervently. "I can't do anything about my loom and the weaving this winter. In fact, unless I buy wool, I'll not be doing much next winter. Since more than half of us hereabouts have been burned out, none will do much for several years until our flocks are built up to strength again. I might as well be helping our cause."

CHAPTER NINE

Benjy Takes Off

THE DAYS stretched into a week, then two. Will Brant did not get well fast. By the last Sunday of October he could do no more than hobble a few steps to a bench using a crutch he had fashioned from a forked branch Benjy had found in the woods. Every day Mr. Brant struggled a few more steps, but then he had to lie back exhausted and in pain. His afternoons he spent polishing the crutch or whittling at a new birch-splint broom for Anna-Mary. His disability put heavy burdens on the rest of the family, especially on Benjy. Sometimes the boy fretted at Melinda just because he was overtired. He did all the fall cleaning up in fields, sheepfold, and barn shed. He took full care of horse, cow, sheep, and chickens. He chopped so much wood that the supply seemed endless; yet his mother was never content with the amount they had in reserve.

The last week of the month was not Benjy's at all. On Monday he spilled a bucket of well water within range of the hearth, putting out the fire and ruining a half sack of cornmeal. On Tuesday he decided not to bother tethering Moomoo. He was sure she'd have good sense and not wander off. But Striker chased the Hawley cat between her legs and the silly cow got so excited that she ran completely off their place and got bogged in the creek mud a mile away. Benjy had to get Tad and Bart Thomson to help rescue her. His father denied him supper and looked significantly at his razor strop.

"Looks like you're fixin' for a good latherin'," he remarked.

Since nothing was wrong with his father's arms and hands, Benjy decided to be more careful.

The next day it poured from morning till night. Melinda soon became bored with her two cornstalk dolls and got pesky. Benjy shouted at her and pulled her hair. In fact, they raised such a ruckus that Mr. Brant hollered for an explanation. Mistress Brant warned, "You'd better mend your ways, Benjy Brant."

Melinda, feeling self-righteous since Benjy seemed to be bearing the brunt of the affair, sat down at the big table and began to play with the candle. She tipped it onto a pewter plate and caught the waxy drippings. Both children did that sometimes, setting little stick and leaf figures they made in the soft wax so that they stood upright when it cooled and hardened.

Benjy, rankling from his scolding, said, "Quit that," with big brother bossiness.

"And why? 'Tain't hurtin' a thing." Melly set up two more stick dolls she had just finished. She tipped the candle again to get more wax. Benjy swung around the table edge to stop her. He bumped her arm. The dried leaf skirt of one of Melly's figures took fire from the candle flame. Melly burst into tears. "Now see what you've done," she cried.

"Aw, quit bawlin', baby," he returned.

Sensitive, the little girl immediately bowed her head into her hands and began to cry. The burning stick figure remelted the wax on the plate, softening it just enough. Melly's long, fine, brown hair swept over the plate as she

snuffled into her hands. In a moment the wax had rehard-
ened and several strands of Melly's braid end were fast in
the dish. She shrieked as the plate bumped on the table.
Benjy burst out laughing at the funny spectacle. His
mother turned around quickly to look. She asked for no
explanation. Getting her shears, she simply cut off as much
of Melly's hair as was necessary. Then she stomped upstairs
to tell her husband that the whole matter was Benjy's fault.
Will Brant roared for his son and grasped his crutch as a
stick.

Benjy wanted to explain but he was too proud to do it.
He walked reluctantly up the narrow stair and stood
abashed before his irate parent.

"I've had enough from you this week," Mr. Brant cried,
and he caught at his son's arm and pulled him within range.
He wielded the crutch stick hard enough against the boy's
behind so that Benjy finally had to yell out loud. "Now,
get out of sight, you hear, get!"

Snuffling, especially with humiliation and the peevish
thought that if he hadn't searched so diligently for the
notched stick it might not have been used against him,
Benjy bumbled across the big bedroom and crawled down
the narrow stairway. He crushed himself into the darkest
corner of his mother's pantry at the end of the cabin and
stayed there. By that time, Melinda, being conscience-smit-
ten herself, tiptoed upstairs and went to stand before her
father, where she made a full confession.

"Did you lick Benjy, Paw?" she whispered, a few
straggly tears stealing down her cheeks.

Her father nodded his head solemnly.

"He's setting in the corner," she confided, "and he's
sore!"

"More inside than out, I expect," her father said. "I'll

talk to him later, since you've told me how it was."

"Hsst! Someone's comin'," sharp-eared Melly cried. Down below the dog growled low in his throat. In a moment he barked. The recognizable and always scary sound of a fist upon the door followed.

A moment later, Mistress Brant opened the door to Captain Lind, who was wet through but in such a hurry that he could only doff his cape and set it to dry a few minutes before the glowing backlog while he went up to see Mr. Brant.

"We're to meet at a designated place day after tomorrow, can you come?" the captain asked bluntly. "I'm rounding up everyone in this area; Peter Horry and Gavin James are taking south and east."

At the vibrant tones of the big captain's voice, Benjy came out of the pantry and stole part way up the back stair to listen. His mother was fixing something hot for the rain-soaked officer. She didn't notice Benjy at all.

" 'Twill be a month or more before I'll be any good at all," Will Brant had to admit. "I have just begun to sit up a few minutes on a bench; miserably confined I am and getting on my own nerves."

"Too bad," the captain said sympathetically. "We hope to raise some little excitement and we'll miss you. I'll be looking back for you later on."

Mr. Brant wished him good luck. Benjy, hearing, ran back down the stairs and hustled out the cabin door before the tall officer came down. It had finally stopped raining. Striker ran out with the boy. Benjy *was* sore, inside and out, and filled, too, with magnificent awe of the captain. Now, if his father couldn't join the patriot cause, Benjy reasoned, he could himself. He was stretching bigger every day and the captain had called him "spunky." He had a young boy's dream of running off and coming to glory, and a good licking certainly burnishes one's ambition for that sort of thing.

Benjy noticed the captain's great black and silver horse tethered at their hitching post. The boy hurried into their dark barn shed; he knew every nook and cranny of it. On cold mornings in winter he sometimes ran out in the morn gloam and shoved Moomoo up from her warm spot and stood in the cozy area her great body had heated to put on his clothes, which he had bundled to warm under his flannel shift. Moomoo was moving around in her stall now. And in the next one Bessie neighed. Stealthily, coaxingly, Benjy got Bessie to back out. He felt for her saddle on its wall peg. Shoving it across her back, with nimble fingers he slipped the girth into the buckle and pulled it taut. Then he led the little brown mare out cautiously by her halter, shooing the nosey dog from between Bessie's legs. He slung their best bridle, which he found easily, too, in his intimate knowledge of the barn, over his arm. Whispering endearments to the horse, he gentled her out and sneaked around the well and through their stubble cornfield out beyond their springtime berry patch.

Still stealthily, Benjy cut a long diagonal northward across Hawley's to where the woods thinned and the Trading Road swung northwest. The captain had mentioned going north. Benjy counted on that.

In the slight open space of the Trading Road, Benjy could see to bridle carefully and he also had enough time. He rolled up the halter and stuffed it in his breeches pocket. He had on a good worsted jacket and new wool socks, but he was hatless and also hungry. Well, his mother had not suggested that the captain stop for a full meal, therefore he ought to be coming soon, Benjy knew.

74

Presently, a crinkling and rustling of brush drew the boy's attention back to where he had himself emerged upon the road. Anxious and expectant, he turned. Striker loped out, gasping a little and stood looking pleasantly up at his young master.

"Drat you! Shoo, get on home, you!" Benjy cried.

The dog retreated into the treeline and stood with a paw raised and one ear cocked. He heard the roll of hooves and then Benjy did, too. It must be the captain coming. Benjy looped his reins over a handy bush and waited for the crucial moment. Soon the dark bulk of the captain's horse appeared. The boy darted out in the nick of time and jumped for the rein at the left side near the bit. He was swung off his feet as the horse stumbled slowing down.

"What the devil!" Captain Lind dived toward the intruder with a rolled fist.

"Captain Lind, suh!" Benjy half screamed.

The officer reined in as the boy dropped his grasp on the horse rein.

" 'Tis Benjy Brant, suh. Paw sez as I could go wi' ye since he can't." This was the bit of business he had carefully dreamed up.

"What?" exclaimed the incredulous captain. "A slip of a child like you. What do you propose?"

"To join ye, suh, wi' Colonel Marion, in Paw's place. I'm a stout one, you said so yourself."

Captain Lind laughed. "Aye, you look stout," he muttered next, staring down at the slight figure in the poor light. "We need men, not babes." He sounded just like Benjy's father.

"I was stout enough and man enough to stop your horse, Captain," the boy snapped with the same spunk he had showed before the British prisoners. His argument was unassailable. "There's few my age would have tried."

Lind laughed again but more seriously. "You've no horse or gun," he protested.

"Here's my horse," Benjy slipped to the roadside and caught Bessie's bridle and pulled her out of the shadows. "I've my gun in the saddle holster."

The captain squinted down at the boy. "How old are you?" he asked.

"Comin' fifteen in spring . . ." That sounded good if the captain did not remember that it was not quite November.

"Listen, my little runt, I mean to ride all night without stopping even to change horse; think what that will mean. I'd beat the soul out of you if you delayed me. At the camp we'll make, ye'll have small cover for winter and little food; and once you've been taken in, no going back. Do you still want to come?"

"Oh, yes, suh, Captain." The boy's eagerness sounded in his voice.

"I don't understand your father letting you go, but I reckon I can give you a bellyful of that excitement you're seeking and still send you home before we get into a campaign of sorts," the captain grinned. "Swing up. Keep your mouth shut. Do as you're told."

A moment later, Lind laid his whip to the rumps of both their horses.

A long time later, Melinda told Benjy what happened at home that night. At deep dark, she smoothed her apron, looking wise, and remarked to her mother, "I know somethin'."

"What now?" Mistress Brant grumbled. "You've been into enough today."

"Benjy's gone!"

"Gone?"

"Aye, he's gone off with that big captain, I *saw* him."

Mistress Brant snatched at their only covered lantern that generally burned constantly in the cabin. She ran out to the barn. It was true, she saw, Bessie was gone and the boy nowhere about. Hot, worried, and angry were the words upstairs in that hour.

"He'll be back," Will Brant muttered finally. "Lind'll not keep the boy, surely. Don't snivel," he added to his wife and Melly, but his own voice was unnaturally thick.

CHAPTER TEN

Some Larking and Testing

CAPTAIN LIND rode the horses almost to death, taking hair-
breadth chances in swamps and full-bodied rivers. Benjy
hung on for dear life without complaining; he had got himself into the thing and he was determined he would see it
through. Before long he was soaked to the skin with ford-
ing; his face was scratched with twigs and briars that
snapped against it; presently, he thought he would go mad
with the relentless anguish of the ride. The captain never
spoke to him at all, certainly never encouraged him but just
rode on and on. Once in a while he struck at Bessie with his
whip, so she'd keep up. The little brown mare ran with all
her faithful heart and Benjy was proud of her.

It must have been near dawn when Benjy knew that he
simply had to stop; he was struggling to sit saddle at all; his
whole body ached. He breathed gaspingly; cold sweat
stood upon his face. He had long ago lost control of the
horse with his legs though he had managed to keep his feet
in the big wooden stirrups which he'd shortened enough.
His legs and toes were numb with fatigue. He shouted to
Captain Lind as they slowed down slightly to cross a brook.

"I can't go on, Captain," he called. "I've got to stop, just
for a minute. I can't get my breath . . . and I've . . ."

The captain's reply came grim upon the crisp before-
dawn breeze. "I've been riding for two days, save for two

hours' stopping. I told you that you couldn't keep up with me, didn't I? I told you I'd give you the devil if you stopped me?" His face was strained and set with his own suffering, the boy could tell.

"I've got to stop; I'm going to stop," Benjy whispered firmly. "I'll try to find you later, suh." He pulled rein slightly.

"Oh, no, you don't! I need every horse I can get, and if you stop here, that horse'll not get on till she's gorged herself on this nice tender outcropping." They were crossing open pasture, green yet under the recent rain. "If you die on her back, you'll not stop her." The captain roared.

"But I must stop! Don't you . . ." the boy began.

Captain Lind reached over and struck him into choking silence with his leather-gloved fist. Tears of pain welled into the boy's eyes. His face swelled immediately from the nasty blow, but he didn't whimper. Lind measured him with shrewd appraisal. Then he struck both their horses with his whip. The animals spurted forward in a last effort.

They had not much farther to go, actually. Just before the thin gray fingers of dawn reached across the dark horizon, the captain turned into a farmyard. Bessie followed the captain's stallion gaspingly. Poor Benjy drooped across her neck, the reins tight in his numb fingers.

"By George!" the captain caught Bessie's bridle as he dropped off his own horse. "I never thought you'd do it, boy," he murmured approvingly.

But Benjy, by then, had suffered too much to appreciate or even to understand the commendation. He made no reply. Another tall fellow came out of the barn before which the captain had stopped. He must have been watching and listening for Captain Lind's arrival. He took the horses' reins and looked curiously at the boy whom Lind lifted down. He had obviously been expecting the captain but not with a youngster.

"Brant's boy," Lind explained briefly. "Take care of him." He went into the barn, a large one with a loft and haymow. He stripped off his outer garments as he dragged himself up to the mow on a rickety ladder. He tossed the pieces of clothing down from the loft opening. "Antoine?" he called to his henchman before rolling to sleep upon the hay, "we needn't leave yet, eh?"

"No, thank your lucky jackboots. No word of any kind as yet. Go ahead and sleep," the fellow shouted back.

Then Antoine began to strip Benjy, whose linsey-woolsey shirt was soaked with sweat. The boy was so drowsy with fatigue that he scarcely recognized what was happening to him. After the tall stranger had bundled him up in a blanket, he made him swallow a cup of hot sweet cider to warm him inside. Then he carried him loftward and deposited him beside the captain already snoring in the hay. The boy was sound asleep from exhaustion before he was entirely tucked into the fragrant hay.

At about four o'clock, Captain Lind awakened and bellowed for his friend. Benjy stirred faintly and buried his face in the crook of his arm. The captain lifted the boy's head in his big hand and looked at his face. Benjy's upper lip was swollen and bruised. "Antoine!" the captain bellowed again.

The fellow came up the rickety ladder vigorously. "Where'd you get that? and what do you plan to do with it now that you have it?" he inquired, nodding toward the sleepy boy.

"I suspect he ran away from home, and I think I can convince him to run right back," Captain Lind explained. "He's a plucky one though; he stuck on that horse of his father's through thick and thin. I intend to keep the horse . . ."

"And how will the boy get back?" Antoine wondered.

"With Mistress McManus' donkey, perhaps? How about some food, man, I'm starved. You'd better rouse this child and feed him, too. What's it doing outside?"

"Raining," Antoine indicated his wet cape and hair.

"Good, Benjy here needs a bath from that sweaty ride; douse him in the downpour and rub him down," the captain ordered. "That should wake him up."

That was exactly what Antoine did. But first he waked the boy gently, talking to him. A half hour later, Benjy came timidly into the big kitchen of the farmhouse where they had halted. Here he was welcomed by a buxom matron, who fed him stew and bacon and corn pone to his heart's content. Captain Lind had finished his own meal and was toasting his feet at the fireplace. He looked the boy over keenly.

"About ready to go home, boy?" he asked, finally. "Sorry I had to hit you like that but I decided that we could use your horse after I'd got it that far."

Benjy looked at him ruefully and put his left hand to his mouth. The hot stew had helped the swelling; so had the bath Antoine had given him in the chilly autumn rainstorm.

"I don't want to go home," Benjy stated quietly. This wasn't exactly the truth; he would have given almost anything to have been that moment back home again on good terms with his family. But he had too much pride.

Lind set his feet down, swung around, stood up. He looked Benjy over again, this time curiously. " 'Tis no life for the likes of you, the one that we're expecting," he observed. "Can you shoot that rifle that you evidently lifted from your old man?"

"Yessuh, I can shoot pretty good, 'specially with a rifle . . . 'tis my own rifle and the second one I've had. My first rifle was stole by a British officer during the sheep trouble . . . I ain't very good wi' a musket."

The big blond captain laughed and nodded at Antoine who was scouring boots. "Who is?" Lind muttered.

A sudden scratching came upon the kitchen door. Mistress McManus, the woman of the house, opened the big door in. A loping yellow dog, big-boned, came in, his sides caving under hard breathing, his tail hanging wearily. He cocked his straw-colored ears high, went directly to Benjy, and laid his muzzle on the boy's knee.

"Striker, you durned fool!" the boy cried. "He . . . he must've follered me," he said a bit stupidly in his surprise. " 'Tis my dog and he follered me all the way."

"Made fair time, I'd say," Antoine observed.

The dog shook himself before the fire. Benjy would have offered him what remained of his stew but the widow McManus found a trencher of scraps. The dog bolted the food eagerly.

"Well, that settles it," Captain Lind announced. "The rain's stopped and I'll put a blanket on Mistress McManus' donkey and you can take your mutt and go home, boy."

"No, suh," Benjy returned with equal firmness. "I ain't goin' home; my paw said I could join ye."

The captain leaned across the table and pinched his ear. "Your paw said what, boy?"

"That I could . . ." Benjy bit his sore lip as the officer's fingers pinched wickedly.

"What did your paw say?" the captain repeated.

Tears of pain rose in Benjy's eyes.

"Answer me straight, boy, or I'll thrash you good before I send you back!"

"I . . . ran away," Benjy admitted. " 'Cause Paw ain't been the same since he was hurt, I guess on account he can't do all the things he wants. I don't want to go home, please, Captain, I don't want to . . . not without havin' done somethin'."

The captain just snorted through his nose. "You take your big clumsy dog, boy, and go on, now that it's clearing."

"No, suh! and Striker'll be no trouble; he can eat on me; he's a good dog . . ."

"We'll be put to it to mind ourselves where we're going, boy, we'll have no dogs. Our own comforts will be small enough," the captain rose, pulled back the bench on which Benjy sat and hauled the boy to his feet. "Come on, I've had enough nonsense."

"I follered you once, I can do it again," Benjy threatened with surprising boldness. He met the captain's steely eyes firmly enough.

"I'll have no dog, boy, send him home!"

Benjy swallowed hard a couple of times, but he took this as compromise. If he got the dog to go home, he could stay! He fastened his fingers at Striker's neck and pulled him outside. He dragged him, somewhat resisting, to the rail fence that marked the farmhouse yard. "Git on home, you!" he cried; and he pointed.

Striker went obediently a little way south, then turned around, sat down, whined.

"Git on!" Benjy shouted.

The dog loped farther, looked back again, turned and went on. The boy came back to the kitchen where he resumed his seat on the bench though he moved about nervously. Captain Lind did not look at him. Five minutes later a familiar scratching drew attention to the door.

"I'll shoot the dog before I have him with us," the captain stated emphatically.

Benjy gulped. Grabbing at the dog, he pulled him outside and went through the process of setting him toward home again.

"Captain, that's a persistent child," Antoine observed.

"He'll take the dog and go home," Lind said confidently.

Sure enough, after two more unsuccessful attempts with Striker, which considerably roused the captain's short temper, Benjy did consent to take the mule and the dog and set off south. The rain had cleared away and the sun was drying the mud rapidly. The boy sat astride a heavy blanket and held the dog before him. The mule, unlike many of its kind, was amenable and happy to get out after a long stay in barnyard and pasture. It trotted along amiably at a fair pace. Striker really had no desire to walk, for the pads of his paws were still sore from his long, speedy trek up. He sat close in the crook of Benjy's arm content.

After an early supper, Captain Lind and his friend went to bed down again on the soft hay in the barn loft. Near midnight, something woke the sharp-eared Lind, a faint stirring below. He lay awake listening awhile but no repetition of whatever had disturbed him occurred. He went back to sleep. Antoine woke first in the morning. He burst out laughing as soon as he sat up to pick the straw from his hair.

"Oh, shut up," growled the sleepy captain as his friend's raucous merriment roused him. "What ails you?"

" 'Tis full day, and pray, sit up and take notice, my fine captain," Antoine warned.

Captain Lind raised himself on an elbow. Beside him, nestled comfortably in the hay, snoring lightly and evenly, lay

Benjamin Brant with the donkey's blanket carefully laid across his hips.

"Got rid of him, did you?" Antoine chuckled in glee.

The captain shook his head, almost unbelieving; then a moment later, he shook the boy, hard, so that Benjy woke with his teeth rattling in his head.

"So you dared to come back, eh? And what of that confounded dog?"

"I convinced him, I reckon, 'cause he went on mighty disgusted-like wi'out me," Benjy stated stoutly. "Now do I get to go on wi' ye, Captain?"

"Well, I'm not about to take you home myself; but hear me, boy, you are excess baggage with me, and you'd better not make me think of that too often, understand? I don't see the slightest prospect of you being worth your keep; mind that I have said this!" His eyes gleamed cold in the bright morning light.

The boy gulped. Then and there he determined that somewhere, somehow he would prove worth his keep. Antoine, merrier and more sympathetic than the stern captain, rubbed the boy's head in a gesture of friendship.

"Since we're saddled with you, you had better know what's what," Lind said. "You keep your mouth shut at all times unless you're asked a question, is that clear? And you stay handy, no running off to explore. This is Lieutenant Antoine DuMonseau, my scouting partner; we're both at present under the command of Colonel Francis Marion, of whom you've heard your father speak and whom you saw that night in the cabin when we hauled you in. Colonel Marion will be looking for trouble, and no tuppence boy will interfere with his operations." The way Captain Lind said this brought back to the boy that terrible night at Congers when he had lost his rifle. Deep in his pocket, Benjy still carried the sixpence marking his shame. He shivered involuntarily and hoped the captain did not notice. Lind went on. "I'd leave you here with Mistress McManus except that you'd not like to stay, would you? In fact, you're enterprising enough not to stay; and this spirit of enterprise be the only thing about you I like! I want not to lose you entirely since I owe your father respect for battle well done twice in the past. You will understand, then, that you must obey me to the letter, boy."

"Yes, suh, I will," Benjy promised, remembering quickly the fist in his face.

"Now then, you will go off with the lieutenant and demonstrate what you can do with that rifle. If you can't manage it, you stay here until I can get someone to take you home . . . if we've to tie you to a bedpost."

"I can shoot," Benjy insisted, not worried. He had hunted enough for his mother when his father was away marketing wool, foraging, or fighting in the not infrequent stirrings of the times.

"Can you also swim?" the captain asked.

"Swim?" the boy asked incredulously, not understanding what swimming might possibly entail for two men talking of war on the edge of winter.

"Yes, swim; if you can't swim, you don't go along either."

"I could learn, maybe," Benjy proposed.

"You *will* learn, today," the captain promised thoroughly.

After eating the good breakfast that Mistress McManus set before him, Benjy went off obediently into a nearby woodsy stretch with Lieutenant DuMonseau. He got along magnificently and brought down a fat grouse and a rabbit. The gay Antoine quickly put him at ease. In fact, the lieutenant let Benjy in on a secret. He had set a pile of bumpy rocks under the hay in the loft just about where the captain usually sprawled for his nap.

When the lieutenant and the boy returned from their shooting practice and hunting, Captain Lind was sitting in the big farmhouse kitchen with a bundle of maps unrolled before him. He made no mention of rocks. Benjy was disappointed. Perhaps the captain had not taken a nap? The boy was so curious that he finally went out to the barn to see if the stones were still laid. They were gone.

They all lunched on fresh pone and milk, Mistress McManus' potted corn and Benjy's fat grouse. Then for two hours the officers pored over the maps while Benjy sat quietly in a corner. He was glad when Mistress McManus gave him a basin of lima beans to shell.

Promptly at three o'clock, Captain Lind rolled up his maps and tied them in an oilskin. "All right, Toni," he suggested, "let's give some swimming lessons."

They went along the creek behind Mistress McManus' farm until the small stream ran a bit wider between two hills. The captain mounted the slope on their side of the stream. The hill formed a little ledge at the top; below the creek widened into a fair-sized pool.

"Take off your clothes, boy," the captain ordered but he did not remove his own.

Benjy stripped and stood shivering a little, more with fear of what was to happen to him than with cold, for the sun was bright and hot. The captain eyed the boy from top to bottom; he even turned him all around. Benjy was a sturdy boy, not plump but evenly fleshed and of a fair height for his age. The captain pulled a bit of string from one of his pockets and tied the loose hair in Benjy's neck high and tight.

"Now, listen to what I tell you. You hold your breath under the water and keep your eyes open. You hear? Repeat what I said," Lind directed.

"Hold my breath under the water and keep my eyes open," Benjy muttered hesitantly, hoping he would remember when the moment came.

"Strike out with your arms, so, one after the other, when your head breaks out of the surface; comb the water, thus, and then kick your feet for dear life. Understand?"

He didn't, but he answered affirmatively. The times he had dared to say "no" to Captain Lind seemed quite decidedly over and he knew it.

"All right, Toni, you take the right side," the captain called.

Before Benjy could wriggle, had he tried, the two men had grasped him simultaneously by his left and right forearms and his legs above the knees. They swung him out a couple of times in a rather sickening swoop. Then the captain called, "Keep your head down so you don't strike the water on your belly!" Benjy was suddenly floating through the air with the greatest of ease straight down toward the pool below the hill ridge like a plummet on a string. He was too frightened to change position very much and so he went in head first and came up quickly. He couldn't remember what the captain had said upon the shock of his entrance into the water; but instinct made him thrash at the cold water with both arms. In a moment he did remember to kick a little, and he managed to flounder about in center pool for several seconds. Then he panicked and went under and came up. He gasped for air too soon and gulped water sickeningly. He tried hard to remember what he should do.

Captain Lind waited calmly until the boy went under a second time and Antoine stepped anxiously near the edge of the hill ledge. But then the captain, who had in the in-

terim stripped off boots and stockings, jumped off the ledge
at the hilltop and landed thigh-high in the edge of the
stream with a splash that wet him rather thoroughly. He
had only to reach out a long arm for the boy to haul him
in, choking and sputtering. He set him at arm's length to
drip.

"You're not worth the salt to season your meat, are
you?" Lind snapped.

"I don't . . . know . . . suh," Benjy gasped, still
choking and sputtering like a half-drowned cat.

"I told you how to use your arms. Now watch and do
what I do," he demonstrated.

The shivering boy imitated him carefully.

"Now run back up the hill," the captain directed.

Benjy cast an appealing look at the water. "Couldn't I
just . . . walk in?" he pleaded.

The captain just pointed to where Lieutenant DuMonseau waited on the hilltop. Benjy went up. They tossed him
in again the same way. He stayed up a little longer but
eventually had to be hauled out again. The third time,
though, he made it, flailing and splashing to shallow water
under his own power. He stood up by himself. The fourth
and fifth times they dropped him feet first. By four-thirty
he could jump off by himself and swim about fifteen
strokes. The captain seemed satisfied with the day's work.

But the next morning Lind himself hauled the boy out of
bed in the warm hayloft at dawn and ran him to the hill
where he made him jump into the icy water before the sun
had peeped over the treetops. However, he stripped off his
own clothes and dived in after the boy and gave him much
more thorough instruction. In the afternoon Antoine did
likewise. By sunset, that second day, Benjy could swim up
or down stream a fair fifty yards. Captain Lind ceased his
derogatory remarks.

CHAPTER ELEVEN

More Larking and Getting Under Way

THE NEXT morning again found the captain up before dawn, but he made no mention of swimming when he woke the lieutenant and the boy. Nothing had ever been said about the stones in the hay. Benjy remembered them curiously but dared not ask either the trickster or the captain.

From preparations the captain made before they left the barn, Benjy gathered that they were going to move on, at last. The captain cleaned out his saddlebags and rubbed down his saddle and curried his horse. He bade Benjy and Antoine do likewise with Bessie and the big chestnut the lieutenant rode. Lastly, Lind changed his North Carolinian line uniform for a woodsman's hunting shirt and trousers, explaining that he was actually a cavalry officer but had served with the Carolinians during the siege and escaped capture.

Later, they all sat down to a fine breakfast of porridge and ham and fried potatoes with hot chocolate to drink. Antoine seemed hesitant about eating his porridge, but Benjy's was just right and he ate it with gusto. The captain seemed to be enjoying his. In fact, David Lind looked squarely at Lieutenant DuMonseau and said, "Wonderful porridge, isn't it? Make the best of it, Lord knows when we'll taste cooking like this again."

"I find mine a trifle salty," Antoine admitted, taking a spoonful of the porridge with a slightly wry expression.

The captain leaned across to his bowl, took a spoonful of the porridge and ate it with a great show of relish. "Delicious," he exclaimed. "Eat up; let me warn you that there'll be days when you will long for a nip o' salt, believe me."

"That may be," Antoine grumbled, continuing to make a sour face.

"Come, come, you'd not hurt our hostess' feelings?" At that, Benjy caught a gleam in the captain's eye that was not missed by the lieutenant either.

Antoine ate his porridge, somewhat hard pressed it seemed; but nevertheless, he ate every mouthful.

In a little while they set out, their horses properly saddled and packed. Saddlebags were stuffed with portable provisions of all kinds: jerked ham and bacon, salt, sugar, vinegar, molasses, blankets, some changes of clothing, old linens, bullets and powder. The captain checked everything off on a careful list he had made.

"Looks like we're fixin' for a regular campaign," Benjy murmured to Antoine at one point.

He nodded. "Like's not, boy," he agreed. "Winter's coming, and British scavengers like Wemyss have ruined the country round. We'll need the things we have and anything more we can root out along our way to carry wi' us."

They rode all the brisk morning; at about ten o'clock Antoine pulled rein beside the captain to indicate that he was insupportably thirsty. Must have been something he ate at breakfast, he suggested. They were crossing a bog. Captain Lind eyed the lieutenant thoroughly; then he offered him his canteen. Antoine opened it and took a great gulp of its contents. His eyes very nearly rolled; he choked and spat.

"What's the matter with you? Wasting water like that? The Lord knows how long we'll be crossing this swamp," the captain cried angrily, yet Benjy was sure his eyes were twinkling.

"Confound you! We'll be another hour and you know it, and I'm spitting wool," Antoine handed the canteen back.

"Drink then, you fool. I filled that canteen myself fresh this morning."

"Yes, you did, my fair-haired captain, and I love you for't!" Antoine cried.

"Drink," Lind held out the container.

"I'll go thirsty," Antoine replied.

"No, you won't, my fine friend, not if you know what's good for you. Discomforting a superior officer, eh? Would you? Drink, my man, that's an order."

Antoine took the canteen and pinched his nose shut and took a gulp. Captain Lind sat back against the crown of his saddle and grinned.

"Fludge!" Antoine cried, nearly choking again.

"Drink up, I'd not have you thirsty," the captain continued.

Benjy nudged him timidly. "What . . . what's to do wi' the water?" he wondered.

"Danged full of sulphur it is, that's what!" Antoine snorted and tried to hold his nose again with one hand.

"Yes, and you'll drink every last drop of it, Toni, won't you?" the captain regarded him quizzically with a hand on his hip. "Won't you?"

Antoine gulped and gurgled and spat and tipped up the canteen valiantly again.

"Answer!"

"Yes . . ." this the lieutenant gave out bullishly between a gulp and an expectoration.

"Yes, what?"

"Yes, sir, hang you, *Captain* Lind!"

"Now, now, that was mighty good porridge you downed this morning?"

Antoine nodded. "Aye, with half a pound of salt in it that our commander might well have been able to use more profitably." He emptied the canteen and handed it back dutifully.

"I take it I may look forward to resting easier in the future, Lieutenant?" the captain asked, trying to look serious.

"Yes . . . sir . . ." Antoine ground out, and then he burst out laughing. "I recommend that you look before you leap into bed, Captain, anyhow; since my spirit moves me to evil sometimes."

"Don't worry, I'll look. And be warned that I'm not quite through with you, my prankster . . . stones in my straw, heh?"

"Lord help us!" Antoine cried and nudged his horse.

They went on at a lively pace. Twice they stopped to muster a half dozen other men who immediately joined them. They went southeast, Benjy knew, by the rise and set of the sun. Three days and nights they traveled; chiefly by day during the early part of the trip when they were in Whig country and could stop anywhere for food and a warm barn's sleeping; but the last sixty hours, when they had come to Tory areas where the British troops also roamed, they went more cautiously after dusk.

At length, they arrived, a motley band of about fourteen men, in the camp of Colonel Marion at Port's Ferry. They found an even more motley group awaiting them. The colonel's numbers had swelled to one hundred fifty on call, but of these not more than half lived in camp. The colonel himself was a picturesque figure. He often limped about from group to group, talking, dispatching scouts, discussing reports, bundled against the fall dampness in the part of his blanket that had not been burned during a recent brush fire. The ankle he had broken just before the siege of Charlestown still bothered him, but it never curtailed his activity.

CHAPTER TWELVE

Benjy Proves Worth His Salt

BENJY never forgot his first official encounter with Colonel
Francis Marion. Benjy was scrubbing mud off Captain
Lind's saddle when the colonel limped by, turned, and
came to talk to the captain. Marion noticed the boy who
had been in and out of camp for more than a week but who
had stayed within close range of Lind or DuMonseau.

"What have we here?" the colonel asked, eying Benjy
who pulled his hair behind his ears nervously at this attention. "More children? Can't you get me men, Captain? I've
enough boys."

Benjy felt his face redden in embarrassment. Antoine,
looking up from a batch of sweet potatoes he was roasting
nearby, felt sorry for the boy. Benjy had ridden uncom-
plaining for long weary miles. He had worked hard at
whatever menial tasks the captain had assigned him. Often,
Lind seemed indifferent to the point of hardness in his rela-
tionship with the boy.

"He's a rather special sort of boy," Antoine ventured to
say.

"Ah, yes, the devil's own," the captain snapped. "Loses a
pound of salt at every ford."

This was a sore subject. That very morning, Benjy had
slipped off Bessie mid-stream as they returned from a chase
after a British express rider. As he struck out bravely for

95

shore, he lost to the swift current a bag of salt which the captain had lifted from the messenger's saddlebags. Salt was more precious than money in Marion's camp. Benjy bit his lip and thought, perhaps not without good reason, of the salt the captain himself had wasted in Antoine's oatmeal; of course, in all fairness, it had not been any bagful.

"If 'twere not for the security involved, you might well send such a one as he is home; what use is he?" the colonel demanded, fixing a fierce black eye upon the youngster. "Where'd you get him anyhow?"

Benjy rubbed his hands against his soiled linsey-woolsey breeches, nervously. "I'll . . . I'll get more salt . . . C . . C . . Colonel, suh, if I have to steal some," he blundered thickly.

Marion lifted an eyebrow. "Make no rash promises, boy, lest I be like to hold you to 'em. Who is he?" he repeated to the captain.

"Will Brant's boy," David replied softly.

"Ah, yes, the one who came looking for Hal that night? For a surgeon? I remember him, now. His father's a good man, I had him with me for three months before the siege of Charlestown. Well, you'd better be worth your salt, boy, eh? For your father's sake," Marion warned grimly.

A patrol of scouts cantered in, splattering mud in all directions. The officer in charge had some startling news that set the little colonel's eyes gleaming. The Tories from Nelson's Ferry to Camden had been mustered by Colonel Samuel Tynes and were camped without much natural protection at the Tarcoat Swamp. Besides, they had just been issued new muskets and plenty of ammunition and they had posted no guards. This was the very thing for which Colonel Marion had been impatiently and grumpily waiting. He called for an immediate muster of his own men. Discovering that he could count upon one hundred and fifty well-prepared followers, he crossed the Peedee River and set up his march.

Lind, along with other of the more experienced and daring captains, wove in and out of the main body, checking lines forward and securing more information about Tynes's position and spreading careful rumors that the wily Colonel Marion was headed in quite an opposite direction. Benjy rode behind Antoine so that Bessie could go to a horseless recruit.

"Shall we see some action?" Benjy whispered into the lieutenant's ear as he clung tightly to Antoine's shoulder fringe.

"I expect so; you mind what you're told and try no tricks," Antoine warned. "Action is not likely to be as thrilling as you may suppose."

Benjy suspected this was true; he remembered his father being brought home from King's Mountain. Also, he had lain awake nights in the encampment, listening to the loose talk that rattled around the campfires. Rumor had the British soldiers still burning, plundering, even killing those Whigs who would not pledge firm allegiance to the king. Marion's men, scuttling out at dark and returning at dawn, wreaked a vengeance of their own on known Tories. Some of the stories were harsh. Sometimes Benjy's flesh crawled as he wondered what was before him.

The small brigade rode all afternoon. Just at dusk they came to the Black River where they turned off the highway and forded. Within a few minutes of the little black swift-running stream that the early settlers had called the "Tarcoat" and from which the surrounding swampland took the same name, Colonel Marion called a halt for reconnoiter. Riding down the rough lines, he spotted Antoine with the boy mounted behind him.

"Lieutenant, take that small boy with you and see if you

can spot the enemy camp. Bring me back exact details. Get you down, boy! You may be just the right size to go in close, unsuspected."

Benjy slipped back and slid off the broad rump of Antoine's good chestnut Monsieur. Colonel Marion himself pulled off the boy's queue string and rumpled up his hair to look unkempt. Next the colonel scooped up a palmful of mud and slapped it against the boy's cheek. "Now leave behind one shoe and your jacket," Marion directed. "Somebody gi' him a knife. You can be trusted to say little if they catch you, eh, son?" he asked.

"I'll be quiet as the grave, suh," Benjy promised.

"Get on with the business then."

Benjy was proud he had been chosen. The lieutenant took a rifle, that was all. They split up almost immediately. Benjy ran in alone from the roadside and hid behind scrub brush on the near end of the British encampment. Antoine went farther up the road, having carefully instructed the boy to circle as close as he could and then get back to the main body of Marion's men by himself. This would prevent them from being seen together; a man alone was always less suspicious.

Before Benjy lay a rough field, evidently long in disuse. Here the young Tory men under Colonel Tynes had made casual camp with their new blankets. A few campfire flickers lit up the thick dusk. Merry voices shouted back and forth. On the fringes of the field, some lads were already asleep, rolled in their blankets on the stubble and crabgrass. Around dull fires, others were still cooking and eating or playing cards and singing.

"Gimme my trick!" Benjy heard. And, "My jack, by gad!"

Hesitant and overly cautious at first, the boy grew

braver as time passed and nobody stirred in his direction. The camp did, indeed, seem to be poorly guarded. Benjy edged from his cover and ran along a broken fence rail to a clump of sumac. Hidden there for a moment or two, he was able to look across the rolling field and make some estimate of the camp's size. The baggage and horses were centered to the rear against the Tarcoat Swamp; this seemed the only precaution toward safety the Tories had taken. The men were scattered across the whole area.

Benjy put his hands in his breeches pockets and ran lightly along the slope of the field down toward the swamp in order to estimate the distance of the left flank of the camp. He attracted no attention until he noticed a man with a musket shining bright and new directly ahead to the right, a sentry Benjy supposed. The fellow turned this way and that but with deliberate slowness. Benjy slid into brush again this time at full length to watch. Had the sentinel heard the thin slop of feet? No, because he swung around and back a few times and then yawned mightily, set down his gun, and sat upon a flat stone with his back to the woods. "Fine sentry!" Benjy thought and dared then to get up and walk even further along. Finally he ducked into a woodsy stretch and skirted the field until he reached the road again. Within moments he had reported back to Colonel Marion. Antoine had not yet returned; but on the basis of what Benjy had seen, the Colonel tentatively divided his little band into three sections: one to veer to the left, another to the right, and the main body to take the center.

Properly divided and disposed, the brigade waited, all three sections in deep silence and patience; even the horses scarcely pawed. Antoine eventually returned with confirmation of all Benjy had reported. The wily Colonel Marion was more certain than ever that his plan of attack was the right one. But he waited until midnight. Exactly then, he drew his men up close, so close in fact, that they could hear the gamblers placing their bets and calling their tricks just as Benjy had heard them earlier. Then, at the silent flash of his pistol as he drew it, Marion himself spurred the attack.

Benjy was relegated to the rear of the center column, along with other younger lads. He was disappointed about this, but afterward Antoine comforted him. It proved to be quite a bloody battle, and what Benjy saw of the field in the gray dawn afterward sickened him. Three Tories had been killed and about fifteen very badly wounded; not much could be done for the latter. The young surgeon that had tended Mr. Brant was not with Marion's brigade at that time. Colonel Marion took twenty-three prisoners, but the British colonel escaped across the swamp as did others of his men who had had the good sense and the cowardice to plunge into the swamp at the first alarm. The best part of the whole business for Colonel Marion was the amount of spoils: eighty excellent horses with brand new bridles and saddles, along with baggage, food, and ammunition.

However, Colonel Marion could not conceal his great disappointment at the escape of Colonel Tynes. He immediately sent out several of his daring officers, among them the bold Captain Lind, all under the leadership of Captain William Clay Snipes. They chased in hot pursuit of Tynes in the High Hills of the Santee.

Benjy remained with Antoine. In the next few days, since Marion marched his brigade back to Kingstree and remained there, resting on his laurels, the militia began to pour in. A success always bolstered the short courage of the militiamen and sent them joining up until the next rough season. Curiously, even some of Tynes's Tories crept out of the swamp and switched loyalties. By this time the shrewd Marion had learned better than to take his swelling ranks as any permanent indication of good fortune. In the back country, it was more common to change loyalty than to show the steadfastness Will Brant had had in time of crisis.

CHAPTER THIRTEEN

A Question of Loyalty

CAPTAIN LIND was not gone half a day when Antoine Du-
Monseau was ordered to investigate a report that one Captain Maurice Murphy was up to his old tricks again. This
Murphy was a self-styled patriot, but he plundered and
burned like the British. Colonel Marion could not abide
him and would undoubtedly have sent a whole party of his
scouts to discipline the fellow except that rumors were easily come by and much exaggerated. Francis Marion would
not attack or punish anyone on mere rumor. Besides, he
saw a chance to catch two pigeons with one stone. Lieutenant DuMonseau could ride down to Lenud's somewhat dis-
guised and discover whether Murphy was actually maraud-
ing near Georgetown as reported; at the same time, he
could stop any supply or dispatch carriers from the British
garrison at Charlestown.

Antoine DuMonseau liked nothing better than an assignment in which he could playact a little. He blackened his
face with swamp muck, and Benjy's, too, so they looked
like two country bumpkins. Then he hitched a mule to a
small cart which he filled with shucked corn. The camp's
supply of corn had just been replenished by incoming par-
tisans. In oddly assorted, borrowed clothes, the lieutenant
seemed no more than a simple fellow seeking a handy
market for some extra fodder. With Benjy as his com-

panion, he posed thus for twenty odd miles; in all that distance the pair of them uncovered no particular adventure.

They crossed the river at Lenud's the next dawn and came down the left bank of the Santee. By full sunup they had not met anyone. They sat down on a gravestone at St. James Chapel and ate hardtack and cold hominy for breakfast.

"Below a short way the Santee road splits near Guercy's and goes out to the coast and down toward Charlestown," Antoine explained to the boy. "I intend to take the Charlestown fork for a mile or so past Chickens' plantation and see what we can see."

It was a crisp morning; even the mule needed little urging. Again they met no other riders coming or going until they heard some whooping and hollering off on the left side of the road.

"We're already beyond the nearest big place," Antoine said. "Let's hide the cart and mule behind that scrub brush and have a look at what is doing."

The noise became recognizable as sounds of horses, shouting, and the piercing cries of a woman as Antoine and Benjy crept through an overgrown field and up a small rise. At length, they stretched out on their bellies behind the shelter of a fallen log at the crest of the high ground. Before them they saw a sturdy log cabin, its cornfield and kitchen garden. A dozen horsemen had trampled the entire place, ruining what had remained of a late harvest. An old woman stood in the cabin doorway with her arms about two children. An old man was tied to the well pulley and a big brute of a man was peeling his shirt into shreds with a bullwhip. At every lash of the whip the woman screamed and the children whimpered against her skirt, where she hid their faces as best she could. But the old man made no sound at all. A brawny bully in a fancy jacket and flourishing a huge horse pistol soon ordered the man with the whip to pass the instrument to another.

"That's Murphy and that's the way he operates, though I am surprised that he is this far southwest," Antoine whispered beneath his hand.

"Hark," Benjy said, "he speaks."

Captain Murphy roared with an oath at the old man. "And now, 'od's blood! who be ye for, old man?"

"For King George," the old man replied, clearly, even calmly; and he was sixty if he was a day.

Another man, at the captain's downswept hand, continued the flogging. Benjy dropped down the bank feeling sick.

"Do something," he gasped to Antoine.

The lieutenant drew a long breath like a sigh and said nothing.

"Why don't he lie, the old man? Why don't he lie?" Benjy cried then. "Look at those we see change sides every other day . . ."

"True," Antoine said, "look at them! And where are we? 'Tis men like this man, Tory or no, who keep the fires burning, who make the liberty we seek precious. Can't you see that?"

"No!" the boy exclaimed bluntly. It was true that he had never understood his own father nor could he now understand this old man. "Do something, Antoine, can't you?" he whispered again to the lieutenant. Nerving himself, Benjy crept back to the log and looked over it.

Below, the flogger had stopped. Again the old man shouted his defiant "I'm for King George!"

"Can you bide quiet as a church mouse no matter what; though I be killed by our own side, so to speak?" Antoine answered softly.

Benjy stared at him.

"I mean that; they'll not take interference in this matter kindly. Answer. This Murphy's killed his own kin at a flash of defiance. Will you go hide with the mule and not move till dark, if I don't return?"

Benjy swallowed hard, then nodded. Antoine gestured him to crawl down the slope. This was not much to the boy's liking; it was hardly interesting to send a rescuer into the fracas below and not see what resulted. But he went down as he was told. That is, he went down until Antoine disappeared out of sight below the hilltop.

Then Benjy promptly turned about and crawled back on his belly until he could again peek over the log. Antoine was already halfway down the slope, careening into the hubbub around the cabin as though he were drunk on applejack, singing a gay French song. Even so, it took several moments before anyone noticed him. For Captain Murphy, at length impressed by the fortitude of the old Tory homesteader, had for some minutes stayed the flogging. He was, instead, issuing orders to his men to ransack the house. Some of his subordinates finally saw Antoine and pointed him out. Two rode up to accost him. He put on a fair show of being a fool idiot. They amused themselves by ordering him to dance.

Quickly, the clever Antoine became so diverting that no one fired the torches that Murphy had ready to light. The old Tory still hung by his wrists and the so-called patriots amused themselves tearing up feather beds and pillows and shaking them out upon Antoine, who frolicked like a child among the feathers until Benjy forgot the seriousness of the whole business and laughed almost loud enough to be heard. Startling himself, he remembered and choked his mirth in his fist. He tried then to hear what went on below.

Quite unexpectedly, Captain Murphy wheeled his big

bay horse, eyed Antoine fiercely, and ordered two of his men to drag him to his stirrup. He leaned down close. Just enough breeze existed to bear what he said clearly up the small rise. "You be putting on an act! Who are you?"

Benjy's heart flipped. But Antoine seemed perfectly calm and in his most devilish manner he must have replied something placating because Murphy roared with laughter, slapped his thigh, and then waved his men to gather round. Benjy shoved off from the log and set himself to rolling all the way down his side of the hill. He soon crashed into high weeds below, and he was not too early getting into the underbrush where the mule was picking at mulberry leaves, for presently the guerrillas came whooping down the hillside not far from the path Antoine and Benjy had chosen to take up their observation point.

Benjy stroked the mule between the ears to take his mind off his appetite for the munching was noisy. Checking Murphy's men as they came down, Benjy counted fourteen. It was possible that several others had ridden on the far side of the slope out of his range of vision because he had originally counted seventeen in the homesteader's yard. He puzzled about the missing men, but all he could do was wait, impatiently.

After what seemed an hour, Antoine appeared on the hilltop. He had washed his face and was coolly eating an apple. He beckoned to Benjy to come out of hiding as soon as he knew the boy could see him. Leading the mule and guiding the cart, Benjy picked his way to where the undergrowth was sparse.

"Come along, they'll give us lunch. We needn't tell our politics; they think I'm as good a Tory as they are," Antoine said.

"Whatever did you say to that Captain Murphy to get him to call off his men?" Benjy asked in all innocence.

"Aha! So that's how you obey your superiors, eh?" Antoine demanded.

Benjy reddened.

"And if it had been Captain Lind you flouted so brazenly, where would ye be? D'ye know?" Toni grinned at him.

"Flogged myself," Benjy hazarded.

"Nay, on your way home and for good, that's what! You had better mind your manners and do as you're told, my boy," Antoine warned and meant it, Benjy knew. The boy resolved to be more careful in the future, especially if the captain was along.

After they had eaten corn dodgers and beef and bacon with the old man and his wife and their grandchildren, Antoine told how he had gotten rid of Murphy.

"I just told him that I was one of Marion's scouts and that Colonel Balfour had sent a detachment of Hessians up from Charlestown who might arrive any moment," he said.

Benjy grinned at the part that was true because the old Tory did not, of course, believe any of what Antoine had said at all.

"Be not this Colonel Marion the commander of this Murphy?" the wife asked.

"No, I think not," Antoine said earnestly. "For whatever Colonel Marion represents to loyal subjects of King George, he is not one to oppress the poor, or to be ruthless and cruel, mark me on that. This Murphy is an exception to the concept of liberty the so-called patriots have embraced . . ."

The old man looked over at him keenly. "I know not," he muttered. "Ye be not one to shift sides, young man?" he asked as his wife changed a wet dressing on his torn shoulders.

"Hurry up, boy," Antoine said to Benjy. "Let's be on

our way." Antoine did not remind the old homesteader that he had never claimed to be Tory.

On the road again with a warm midday sun beating down upon them, Benjy found the day pleasant, peaceful, and quiet. The thing they had just witnessed seemed like a dream. Then just before they crossed the Charlestown pike, Benjy brought up something that bothered him.

"Lieutenant," he said, "why did that old man not lie and say he was for Congress and the patriots? How would Murphy have known different?"

Antoine shook his head. "Firstly, Murphy may well have had a list of patriots from a county register and seen that Mr. Brynne's name was not on it. Such lists . . . or their counterparts, listings of Tories . . . are passed from time to time into the wrong hands for sundry reasons. And secondly, I daresay Mr. Brynne did not lie for the same reason ye tell me your own father did not."

"Ye lied yoursel' to this Murphy! Ye told him only a part of the truth and also a gross untruth about Balfour and the Hessians, when your neck was in danger," Benjy accused.

"That's different. All's fair in love and war, they say. I was acting the spy, out of uniform, a dangerous business where dramatics and lying are implements of the trade," Antoine explained.

"I don't understand any difference," Benjy insisted.

"There is one, nevertheless, and you must needs understand it. Put it thus: this Mr. Brynne that they flogged, he was at peace in his world, a loyal subject of his king; he wanted no part of the quarrel. But he was forced to stand upon his belief at his hour of trial. So was your father. For either one to have lied would have saved his skin only until he was found out, for one thing, and it would have been dishonorable, for another. A spy lies as part of his duty, not merely to save his skin but to accomplish a larger purpose. Even so, he can claim no honor in the eyes of his enemies. Do you understand this?"

Benjy promptly replied, "No." He trudged silently at Antoine's side for a quarter mile, thinking. Suddenly, he asked, "If you were in your uniform, would you lie as a spy?"

Antoine smiled. "Clothing does not make any essential difference, Benjy. As a spy I might or might not lie depending on the circumstance, no matter what I wore. How many of Marion's men have any part of a uniform to begin with? Oh, Lor', boy, you be hardheaded! Put it thus, as a Carolinian and a patriot backed up against the thin wall between life and death, I pray God I should have the courage not to lie. Can you understand that?"

Benjy said, "No, because though my father be alive, our sheep are dead, and we could as leave starve to death . . . and I couldn't see his purpose and I still cannot . . . for all I know they be starvin' home now . . ." This bitter thought haunted him at night. "How much more might Paw have gained for a little baby of a lie?" he wondered.

" 'Tis not a thing you can touch with your hand," Antoine frowned and shrugged. " 'Tis deep within and a thing of the spirit . . ." He could see that the boy spoke truly about not understanding.

CHAPTER FOURTEEN

Off with Captain Lind

BACK AT Marion's encampment the next few days, no one settled very long at anything. The colonel sent his trusted scouts out in small forays in all directions spying, foraging, rendezvousing, patrolling. No British supply wagon was safe along the great length of the Santee Road. The despatchers in Charlestown were soon forced to order their wagoners to Camden by way of Friday's Ferry on the Congaree, a very long way around. No messenger was safe nor any small party of Tories.

No one liked this type of service better than Captain Lind, who had come back from a successful expedition. Colonel Tynes had been captured and his militiamen were safely confined in a prison camp in North Carolina. And it was Lind who had intercepted a despatch from Colonel Balfour to Lord Cornwallis in which the Colonel complained of "the numbers & spirits of the rebell partys" so far outbalancing the Tory militia that a post must soon be established near Kingstree.

Of course, the British had out patrols and spies, too; and they bribed the vacillating country folk who swayed under each favorable wind.

"If there are to be any amount of the enemy's military sent down from Winnsborough, I would know about it," Colonel Marion said, reading the intercepted message.

And so Captain Lind volunteered to go up the Wateree River and across to Camden if need be to see what he could find out. He planned to meet Antoine at Beach Creek below the Howard plantation and set as a tentative date the afternoon of November fourth. The exact rendezvous point was to be an old millhouse at the conjunction of the creek and the Santee highroad. This would be within several hours' ride of where Marion was busily assembling more and more troops around Singleton's Mills. After some debating for and against, the captain decided to take Benjy with him. Bessie held the captain back considerably, for his great black and silver stallion Hamlet could ride like a storm; but the boy alone on the high road would not be as suspicious-looking as the captain alone. More than once Lind found it convenient to melt into the roadside brush or step Hamlet into the edge of a swamp while Benjy settled Bessie into a slow jog until the approaching stranger hailed and passed him.

One time it was a blacksmith's apprentice delivering a just-shod farm horse; once it was an elderly man going to visit his son; and the third time it was a soldier in a red coat and buff breeches who neither stopped nor spoke. Instead, he slapped his horse and used his spurs. The instant he was past, Captain Lind broke out of cover and fifty yards ahead he brought him down.

Benjy had not got past the next bend when the captain came, easy in the saddle with the Britisher's despatch case and his pair of horse pistols, his bridle, saddle blanket and silver spurs. The latter he gave to Benjy as a souvenir.

"Did you kill him?" Benjy asked.

"No, but he drew on me and I lamed his right arm and left him with a bridleless horse. If he heads in the right direction, he'll find a house to take him in."

"Should you not have taken him prisoner?" Benjy wondered.

"Why? He has no information for me or for the colonel; he would be naught but a burden to us," the captain replied.

A little farther on, the captain picked up rumors that Colonel Banastre Tarleton and his Green Horse had descended from British headquarters at Winnsborough and were actually riding down the Santee Road.

"Last report we had at Marion's camp was that he was sick abed with malaria and half the British staff officers besides," the captain protested to the patriot farmer who had informed him.

The man assured him that the British cavalryman had recovered from his illness and been sent out by his commander-in-chief to "put an end to the exploits of that Mr. Marion!"

"I'd better be sure," Lind whispered to Benjy after agreeing to have a bit of supper with the farmer, "for if Tarleton is on the way, 'tis a different face upon the whole situation and more than doubles the importance of our mission."

Benjy's neck pricked under inner excitement. And after they had eaten and set out into the still, crisp night, he grew more eager. Man and boy, snug in good hunting shirts and looking harmless, rode up the highway as far as Town Creek. A half mile beyond they found themselves approaching a ramshackle tavern. A clink of metal and the squeaking of saddle leather alerted Captain Lind immediately. He took Hamlet and Bessie off the road behind some scrub oak and scraggly pine.

"Go on foot as far as you can get without being seen and just listen," he directed Benjy. "If you cannot find out anything, come back, and I'll go."

When Benjy had come within thirty yards of the inn-yard, a serving girl came out with a lantern, opening the door wide enough so that he could see some of the men inside as well as those gathered about the horses in the court-yard. Those outside were militia clad in a nondescript manner but they were well-mounted upon fine horses; inside were groups of green-jacketed dragoons—Benjy recognized their cavalry sabers and their tight leggings. As soon as the boy reported to Captain Lind, he was ordered to watch the horses. Lind went up to the tavern himself and returned shortly.

" 'Tis true, the rumor about Tarleton. The militiamen by their speech seem local and may be Major Harrison's. I like not the idea of Harrison guiding Tarleton, for his men know every pebble, bush, and swamp of this country," the captain said. "Let's go back," he added, "we know enough."

They rode back as they had come, twelve miles. Then the captain left the road and found a convenient haystack. He fed the horses from a tow sack of fodder he had brought along, hobbled them with rope hobbles, threw Benjy the blanket he had taken from the British soldier and rolled up in his own. They slept on the sheltered side of the hay, snug and quiet beneath the stars.

At the crack of dawn, the captain arose and took the horses to drink at a nearby stream. He shared crumbly corn pone and several handfuls of dried peas with Benjy; they drank their fill at a little spring. Before full daylight had colored the east, they were on their way again, southeast.

"Hear me, boy," the captain cautioned suddenly, slowing Hamlet to a pace that was comfortable for Bessie. "This Tarleton, I know him . . . he has the speed of a devil and for all we know what we took for his vanguard at the inn above may be his rearguard by now. I've known him to ride his horsemen all night and put 'em into battle as fresh as daisies at dawn."

"Is he a butcher as they say?" Benjy asked.

Lind cleared his throat. "You've heard that, eh? I know not actually, he's bold and daring and as a commander he allows his men a license I could not. He lets them go, d'ye understand, when it suits his purpose, and they run wild, and I suppose they like him for't; and when luck puts him in a tight spot, they do his will. Therein lies his ugly reputation. I was at the Waxhaws, I saw what happened . . . Antoine has a slash as long as my forearm down his right thigh into which one of Tarleton's surgeons stuffed tow and let him lie."

"Was that bad?" Benjy asked innocently. " 'Tis what we save for bleedings in the back country, Maw keeps a bucket o' the flax and the wool combings as tow . . ."

Captain Lind laughed. "Not the doctorin', boy, true enough we were lucky they did any, but the Americans begged quarter at that battle and got none."

Benjy nodded. "I know, my uncle was killed there and that's why the password at King's Mountain was Buford."

"Hear me now, should we be taken, I shall try to set you apart, understand? And I'm giving you the papers now; if you can, get them to Antoine, understand . . . and say nothing. I repeat *say nothing* to anyone. You know nothing, have seen nothing. You do not know me or my name or how I came here, understand?"

"Yes, suh," Benjy muttered, but his mind whirled. Why such directions, he wondered. He remembered sharply that Captain Lind wore no uniform and carried no identification, although under the rules of war, if he were carrying a legitimate message on the high road, he would be entitled to the privileges of a prisoner of war. He thought of how

Lind had treated the soldier he had captured the day before. He worried a little and felt a small pang of homesick-
ness.

A sudden clomp-clomp was borne on the morning
breeze behind them. The captain struck Bessie's flank with
the flat of his gloved hand and pulled up his own reins. At
the first open field before a small wood, he turned off,
spurring so fiercely that Hamlet's hooves churned up the
winter hardened soil. Horses, man, and boy melted into the
woods just in time. A small troop of nondescript militia and
smartly dressed green, black, and buff dragoons rode by.

" 'Od's fish, they're everywhere, unless those be our
friends of the tavern caught up, which I doubt," the captain muttered.

He took to the river bank almost immediately. It was a
longer, more circuitous and more treacherous route, but
Captain Lind was used to swamps and so was Hamlet. Off
the beaten path, it seemed safer, too. Just before noon they
arrived on the north shore of Beach Creek and followed it
to the millhouse rendezvous. It was deserted. Antoine had
not yet arrived.

The mill had not been used for some time. The sluice
gate was open, however. The mill wheel turned but the
millstones were not connected. An eerie monotony of
rumbling sound accompanied the splashing of the wheel
and the unused energy it generated. Beyond the wheel-
room, a large room with a huge stone fireplace proved still
comfortably weatherproof. Woodsmen, hunters, scouts
had undoubtedly frequented it. In one corner it had a jack
bed with rope springs and a very soggy cornhusk mattress.
Scraps of dried food, a bent tin cup, several wooden
trenchers lay on a long pine table. A couple of tree stumps
served as stools. Some thoughtful temporary occupant

had even piled up a bundle of faggots against cold and then not entirely used them up.

"Have you been here before?" Benjy asked after he had carefully hobbled their horses in a sheltered spot and come inside.

"Aye," the captain admitted. "Look you, should we be rooted out . . ."

"Why should we be?" the boy interrupted, though he might have known that what the captain knew of the place, others could also know.

"Hear me!" the captain swung at him and pulled him round by a forelock. "Drat you, boy, you are forever wool-gathering. For any clever scout or even a sharp cavalryman we have left a trail, mark! A roundabout one, difficult to follow quickly, but nevertheless plain to an experienced eye. 'Tis impossible to hurry and cover a trail; I have hurried, for I would get down to the colonel with our news. I shall not wait beyond sunset for Antoine. Now, let me warn you again, should we be discovered, and I think it not at all unlikely, yonder in that wall beside the 'place, look sharp! See the pegs to make a ladder?"

Benjy saw where he pointed at the right of the fireplace.

"The top board above is loose. Climb up and see for yourself; it leads to the hopper room but through a little closet barely big enough for a man. I know not its purpose if it has any, but 'tis a dandy place for a boy like you to hide. Do you get into't if we be disturbed. And put the papers I gave you under your shirt next to your skin and guard them with your life, for they could hang us both, mind!" Having said all this, Captain Lind sat down calmly at the table and began to dole out a dozen dried figs from one of his saddlebags. "Here, eat," he said, "and then take my canteen and fetch us some water. If we be not disturbed, I'll make us a fair stew of jerky and sweet potatoes for supper . . . to delight that lieutenant of mine . . ."

Benjy had gone over to test the peg ladder.

"Up wi' ye, boy, and try the opening," the captain encouraged.

The loose plank was certainly narrow. Benjy had to squeeze to get through. Then sure enough, he found himself in a narrow, coffin-like closet with thin shelves along its back wall. Very likely, the thing had been designed to give easy access to the mill room in bad weather or an emergency. The miller must have been a slight man or else only his youngest apprentice made use of the device. Benjy opened the closet door and blew out some of the accumulated dust. Later he was glad that he had.

CHAPTER FIFTEEN

Of Lying and Spying

CAPTAIN LIND spread his own blanket on top of the corn-husk mattress and stretched out while Benjy wandered around outside exploring the millyard and watching the mill wheel turn. The wheel was badly in need of repair, cup paddles were missing, moss thickened on the race. Mud and sticks clogged the entrance of the water at the pond end of the sluice. Benjy amused himself balancing on the race ledge, a precarious sport, for it was slimy with wet moss and algae. Later, he returned to the big fireplace room.

The captain heaved himself toward the wall and made space for the boy beside him. Benjy noticed that Lind had left almost everything with Hamlet, all the items he had lifted from the British express rider; except for his own blanket and the provisions he had not taken anything out of his saddlebags or from his saddle roll. Benjy thought this odd but he said nothing. A two-day growth of beard made Lind stubble-chinned and rough-country looking. The only thing which belied this appearance was the fact that his boots were of good leather and cut like a cavalryman's, fitted with doeskin tops that laced about his thighs. Times were when he changed these, too, for moccasins, but on this trip he had not done so. Benjy clasped his fingers behind his head. His eyes wandered to the peg ladder. He wasn't a bit sleepy.

Neither was the captain because presently he spoke softly to the boy. "Benjy, I would tell you something else to remember. When you were out with Antoine and Murphy flogged old Mr. Brynne, do you remember what Antoine did? He feigned to create a disturbance, an interruption . . ."

Benjy nodded.

"Yet he never identified himself; also you were safe and free the whole while, remember?"

"Yes, suh."

"Well, that's the advantage of trailing in pairs, you see. Sometimes I admit 'tis better to be alone but often enough 'tis better to have a partner in the mischief."

"I see," Benjy said.

Then the captain laid a restraining hand upon his arm. They tensed together at the unmistakable sound of dry branches crackling. Someone was approaching along an overgrown path.

"Up wi' you and not a sound!" The captain boosted the boy toward the peg ladder.

Before he slipped the plank back into its place behind him, Benjy saw Captain Lind return to the coarse bed again. He sat down upon it coolly alert to the sounds outside. With an ear to the plank, Benjy learned quickly that it was a party of men, for sounds of talk, more crackling, the whinny of a horse were all identifiable. Benjy knelt carefully on the loose plank to listen. The oilskin packet of papers rested secure under his knit red belt. Below the door was flung in. Captain Lind shouted out.

"Holloa!"

"In the king's name, who be you?" a voice demanded.

"Why in the king's name, this be Carolina," Lind replied boldly.

"Are you a demmed rebel then?"

"Not I," he returned. "I be Aaron Ward of Kentuck'
. . . come to investigate this abandoned property of my
mother's uncle." He was going to bluff it boldly.

Who were the intruders, the boy wondered? British
army or loyalist militia or just cautious country folk talking loyal because the rumor of the British troops descending from Winnsborough had spread like wildfire?

"Ye're a king's man then? And ye'll take an oath to't?"
the first man who seemed chief spokesman asked.

Surprisingly, Lind said, "Mayhap I'll take oath, yea, but
I be no man for partisanship, you mind."

For a moment no one spoke, as though such an attitude
as Lind had just expressed gave the company pause.

"Be you armed?" a different voice asked next.

"What man travels alone in these parts unarmed?" the
captain was still bold. "I've my rifle there beside the 'place,
my hunting knife and an ax." These were what he had
brought into the millhouse along with his canteen and the
sack of provisions.

"Be that all? No horse or mule?" the questioning voice
continued.

"My horse be above to a blacksmith for want of a shoe."
That lie was too glib and too soon said.

A clatter at the door indicated an addition to the visiting
party. In fact, Benjy thought he identified the jingle of
spurs and a clank of heavy arms.

"He lies!" a thick voice shouted. "Disarm him."

Scuffling and scurrying was followed by shouts, the
crash of furniture, cries of pain. Benjy knelt on the plank in
an agony of suspense, afraid to breathe deeply. Were the
sharp cries in response to the captain's terrifying left fist or
to the use of his knife; or were they his own?

"Hold him fast," came the forceful voice again. "And

now, my fine fellow, tell us some truth for a change. This be the man we've trailed all day," the voice announced, convinced. "What say you, fellow," the man was certainly addressing Captain Lind, perhaps with *his* fist as well as his tongue. "What say you to these saddle pistols with GR on them for George Rex, this British bridle, this blanket of the 71st Infantry? What of the despatch carrier ye crippled above and left to flounder through the river bog? Answer this!" They must have discovered the horses, Benjy realized.

"I know naught of what you speak," David Lind stated clearly. Benjy recognized now why he had taken so few items of their baggage with them; he would deny knowing of the horses. Benjy swallowed great gulps of saliva and struggled not to cough in the dusty atmosphere of his box-like hiding place.

"Drag him here to the door. Be this not your horse and that of your accomplice?"

Lind denied ownership as Benjy had known he would.

"Search everywhere. Either he has an accomplice or he has stolen the second horse; look in every nook and cranny," came the commanding voice.

For several moments Benjy could hear nothing from below; he could only suppose the captain held captive by several men, perhaps already bound hand and foot against any more mischief. That he had led his captors a scramble about the big room, Benjy had heard, but now all was surprisingly still. Afraid to draw his lungs full of air, the boy breathed shallowly and crouched against the floor. How hard he prayed that no one would notice the closet. From the upper mill room it was not easily seen because it had no panels and no knob or loop to open it. Soon, Benjy supposed as soon as they had searched outside, the search party came clattering up to the grinding platform, shouting and yelling, three or four men.

Eventually, all the searchers returned to the fireplace room and reported the failure of their efforts. Benjy breathed easier.

"Sergeant," someone said, "if this be the man that stopped Ensign Jules, he should have his papers . . ."

"Have you anything to say?" the sergeant asked.

From the sound of it Captain Lind may have spat at his feet . . . and received in his turn a whack across the face that might have sent a lesser man spinning or howling.

"Get the ensign from the wagon and let's have an end to his dissembling," the sergeant ordered.

Benjy's heart sank. If the ensign identified Lind as his assailant on the road, and he undoubtedly would, that would be an end to it. Truly, Captain Lind might swing from the nearest tree if the officer in charge were so inclined. It took some time, agonizing to Benjy, until the ensign arrived; but when he did, he immediately stated that the prisoner was the same fellow who had attacked him on the road.

"Sergeant," a new voice rang with authority; it was undoubtedly the officer of the detachment, "keep six men of your choice and find out for me what this fellow did with the despatches and what else he knows. I shall be at the Ryerson house supping . . ."

Thus began two hours Benjy never cared to remember. He prayed for the arrival of Antoine, yet in his heart he was glad the rollicking young lieutenant did not appear, for he would surely have walked helplessly into the trap. The loyalist and British party were evidently spread out about the neighborhood like a great net to catch the unwitting.

The sergeant began by searching his prisoner from head

to toe. From the talk Benjy determined that he discovered nothing more incriminating than Lind's penknife with the initials DML and not AW. Would the prisoner admit to his right name and business and tell without further ado what he knew of Ensign Jules's despatch papers? He would not! In fact, Lind must have spat again because Benjy could hear the blows that were rained upon him. Then he was ordered spread-eagled between the bedpost and the legs of the heavy table which the soldiers turned to suit them.

Benjy could not tell what they were doing to the captain, but as the interrogation proceeded and the questions came incessantly, Lind, strong as he was, cursed nastily and then groaned. The boy shuddered in his hiding place; he could not imagine Lind suffering enough to groan.

It became dark in the millhouse. A flare, a lantern, or some other light was presently provided below because Benjy could see streaks of flickering between the cracks in the planks. He noticed a knothole and got his fingernails into it. For a long time he worked to loosen it. The interrogation below continued quite steadily, punctuated by single sharp groans from the captain. Why didn't he demand his rights as a prisoner of war, Benjy wondered. The captain had once told Benjy that he made a fine scout because he could, in a pinch, claim to be a member of the 2nd Virginia Lighthorse; happily on leave at home in Charlestown during the disastrous battle of Camden, he had missed capture. No one could prove him to be one of Colonel Marion's spies . . . as an officer of the Continental Army he would be entitled to imprisonment and exchange. But what was the use of all this if he denied it so boldly as he was doing below? Off and on between the creak of the slow-moving millwheel, Benjy could hear his denials: he had no papers from Ensign Jules, he had no accomplice, he had no assignment, he had never heard of Francis Marion . . . It went on and on. Finally, Benjy got the round knot of wood out of the board. He sat sucking his sore fingertips a moment or two. Then he doubled himself into a bundle and laid an eye to the hole. He could barely see at his odd angle but he was able to make out that the thick thudding sounds he so frequently heard were the boots of a great hulking Irish dragoon who stamped upon first one and then another of the stripped arms of Captain Lind. Benjy could not see the captain's face; the best he could see was his left arm; it was bruised dark from shoulder to wrist. Benjy shuddered.

"You have your hands, man, speak before it is too late," the sergeant suggested next, coaxingly. "Say, at least, who you be truly, and gi' us the despatches."

"No." The negative was firm enough.

The sergeant poised his foot just beyond the cord that bound the captain's left wrist to the table leg. Benjy could bear no more. He tore the oilskin packet from his shirt front. Standing as high as he could, he put it up to the dusty top back shelf of the narrow closet. Then he wrenched up the loose plank with both hands and screamed through the opening.

"Holloa below! catch me if you can; he's lying; he's lying; and I'll tell you true!"

He burst out of the closet and ran across the hopper room as hard as he could, whirling around the platform and the millstones to the rickety downstair. He was not sure what he hoped to accomplish, but he was determined to save the captain's hands, for the moment, by creating a diversion. He succeeded admirably. Practically everyone except the sergeant took off in sundry directions. One fellow spotted the hole through which Benjy had so boldly called, quickly discovered the pegs, mounted them, and then got himself stuck tight at his middle in the opening. He hung there roaring in embarrassment until the sergeant himself hauled him down.

Within minutes though, two militiamen who had been on guard outside caught Benjy running along the race. Since he frequently slipped, they soon overtook him and hauled him kicking and screaming defiance into the big room. Here the sergeant and a corporal who both wore the green and black of the British Legion searched him with poking fingers and shook him thoroughly until he stopped his hoarse yelling and consented to stand somewhat respectfully before them.

"You know this man?" the sergeant asked, pointing his boot toe at Captain Lind.

Benjy looked upon the captain's bruised and bleeding face. He had been roughly used. Undoubtedly some of the damage had been done during the first wild pursuit they had been forced to make of him around the room when anyone's misstep at the wide door might have got him his freedom. Benjy gulped back both feeling and fear.

"Yea," he whispered.

"Who be he then?" the sergeant asked.

"He's a captain in the 2nd Virginia Lighthorse and entitled to the privileges of war," Benjy stated stoutly.

The sergeant laughed and asked, "Thus, out o' uniform?"

Captain Lind cursed Benjy and cried, "Stop! shut your mouth, boy!"

"Nay, I'll tell true," the boy insisted. "He has not the despatch case from the ensign for he gave it to one of Marion's men. He knows not himself where Colonel Marion be, but I know and I'll lead you there . . . if you desist from punishing him and follow me . . ."

"Hush, boy!" Lind almost screamed. The corporal

kicked him in the side and knocked out his breath.

"You know where that skulking Marion lies?" the sergeant asked. "Bah, I don't believe it."

But the captain groaned and cried out as though he were in mortal agony, so the sergeant became curious. "Benjy, betray them not! For the love of God, boy. Sergeant, I tell you, he's mad, I'm no soldier, I had no papers, I gave none to anybody!"

"Let him go," Benjy whispered, moving away as though the captain had strength and means to strangle him for speaking. "And come out before it is full dark or I cannot lead you past the swamps . . ."

"What do you know of this country, boy?" the sergeant was skeptical.

"I was born here above Richbour's milldam, and I've to take you now between Tarcoat and Ox Swamp to find Colonel Marion . . ."

"Shut up!" cried Captain Lind loudly.

The sergeant's interest heightened. "Fetch the horses and we'll test the boy's veracity."

"And him?" the corporal kicked at Captain Lind.

"Let him lie, he's safe tied . . . he can await our pleasure."

Benjy tightened. He had expected they would take their prisoner with them. Though he had no plans for the moment, the boy intended to engineer something en route. But no one made any move to relieve Lind of his agonizing discomfort, no one so much as wet his lips with a sop of water. Within a very few moments, the corporal had brought Hamlet and Bessie along with other troop horses to the door. A militiaman mounted Lind's great black and silver stallion as the sergeant said, "The colonel will want a look at that handsome beast."

A second later, the "handsome beast" had tossed his would-be rider into the millstream. A dragoon tried him next with scourge and spurs. He fared no better.

"Here!" cried the brawly sergeant, "put the boy up and let's see what happens." He chuckled wickedly.

Benjy had small hope of keeping his seat. No one rode Hamlet but the captain; no one dared try. To add to his distress, the corporal tied his hands tightly together before him. Then he lifted him into the saddle after shortening the stirrups as high as they would go. Hamlet rolled his eyes and whisked his great tail, but perhaps he decided Benjy was a better bet than some rough stranger; when the dragoon put the reins between Benjy's fingers and the man at the column's head hollered "Huzza!" the big horse walked quietly and then broke into a light trot. Bessie was appropriated by a militiaman whom she bore with her usual gentleness.

CHAPTER SIXTEEN

Out of the Captain's Good Graces

THE SUNSET had clouded over so it was not yet as close to twilight as Benjy had imagined in his cramped closet. Dampness indicated that there might be a good chance of fog over the marshes when it got colder at night. Benjy thanked heaven for this. Luckily, he had created his diversion early enough to give him the benefit of remaining daylight, perhaps an hour of it. He took the company down the Santee Road as far as Shank's Creek and then cut off on the north bank to follow it closely.

Benjy had noted that the sergeant had not posted a guard at the millhouse but had left Lind alone to live or die as he might. The fact that Antoine had not made his rendezvous gave Benjy both hope and despair. If the lieutenant were merely delayed or cautious, he might yet come though he would have the neighborhood net of British and loyalists to penetrate. If he were dead, that was something else. Benjy dared not think of that.

The corporal sent a trio of men into Westbury plantation to advise their commanding lieutenant and his party of their departure. The word back said that the major group had agreed to rest the night there in comfort. Benjy thought of the condition in which they had left Captain Lind and shuddered. He spent several miles of his ride trying to free his hands but succeeded only in chafing his wrists raw. With care he skirted Ox Swamp on its northern fringe. Then he took the only path he knew through the great pine barrens.

It gradually became dark. The sergeant began to be restless. A wispy fog dropped its curtains of mist here and there about the time that Benjy recognized the shadowy masses of live oaks and the squshy ground of Halfway Swamp. He knew the way through but intended not to use it until he had gotten the British thoroughly lost in the bogs.

After a half mile of most uncertain footing, the sergeant became suspicious. Benjy felt it was time to make his break. Whenever his column companions, two dragoons on each side, were talking, Benjy managed to weaken the thongs on his hands by biting and nipping at them. But he never broke them through. In another quarter-hour it would be too dark to trust himself to the swamp. Sneakily, he edged Hamlet closer toward the swamp border until he had forced his left hand guard almost into the water. Benjy was almost ready, two more yards, three . . .

Swiftly loosing his left foot from the big stirrup, Benjy kicked Hamlet hard in the flank, hollered "Yiiikes!" and plunged headlong to the far left. Hamlet gave him enough of a lurch so that he cleared his dragoon companion's horse. As he hit ground, Benjy grabbed at a bit of broken branch to break his fall. Still clutching the piece of wood between his bound hands, the boy dived into a wide pool of the swamp. He swam underwater with a strong kick, grateful for Captain Lind's strenuous course in swimming. He stayed under as long as he could, surfaced to breathe and flung the stump piece as wide to the left as he could. Even handicapped by the tight binding on his wrists, he managed to toss it enough away. The British dragoons took its noisy plop for Benjy surfacing. They emptied their pistols in that direction. Benjy surface-dived and swam under again another twenty feet. The water was very cold.

Coming up the second time beyond range of everything except the shouts of the British, the boy found himself safely behind a clump of wide live oak. He climbed onto the huge roots protruding from the water and got his breath. He had to chance getting back to the millhouse before the British and Loyalists found their way back to Westbury and assistance. Biting at his bonds and rubbing them against the rough oak stump, Benjy finally freed himself.

He hoped that the enemy would lose their way along the swamp edges or at the Spurlock Branch, perhaps taking that for Shank's Creek. Darkness would now serve him well and the British ill. But being without a horse was a handicap. He set out to cross-country out of the swamp in a wide semi-circle, in case the sergeant went on instead of turning back. Having lost all sight and sound of company, Benjy trotted swiftly along the edge of the pine barrens to dry his clothes. He took off his shoepacks and stuck them in his belt. He could go faster in his bare feet. At no time did he take to the roads. When he came to one, he skirted along its edge, making his turns by the starry sky now. Out of the pine barrens the mist had dissipated under the night breeze. Only once Benjy had to creep into brush and hold painfully still. A patrol of horsemen passed; not any of the men he had tricked, he felt sure, but a well-armed group with sabers and sidearms clinking ominously.

He let them get well out of sound before he broke from his hiding place. Yet he had not gone a half mile when he heard a horse again. Sure enough, a big horse came trotting over the last small rise. Benjy looked carefully. The beast seemed riderless: could it be Captain Lind's stallion who was trained to circle and come back? Benjy put his knuckles in his mouth and whistled in as close an imitation of the captain as he could manage. But he really didn't expect the big horse to stop for him . . . nor did he . . . in fact, the animal went by so fast that Benjy could not be sure it was Hamlet after all. He could only tell with certainty that the animal was without a rider and that the reins hung loose on his neck. Benjy remembered how he had once stopped the big horse . . . if he had been sure this time? He went on trudging as close to the road as he dared.

It was nearly midnight when he cut into a field opposite the Westbury plantation. The house was far from the road. If the British had stationed a guard at the road gate, he was half asleep, because Benjy saw no sign of anyone. If his figuring was accurate, he knew he could follow the left fields on a long diagonal until he struck the soft marshy ground of Beach Creek. Then, if he could find a place to hold his weight, he could get all the way to the water and swim or wade across to the mill, saving all the distance it would take to go around.

His calculations proved correct. Sooner than he expected, he was running along the millrace toward the millhouse. Everything was quiet except for the dripping water and the squeaking of the mill wheel. The boy ran in at the race level on the floor of the hopper room. Going directly to the narrow closet, he reached up and felt for the oilskin packet. It slipped under his eager fingers and bumped him unexpectedly on the forehead. He cried "ouch" and the word echoed in the empty building. Below through the hole came a thrashing sound. The captain was alive at least though still bound helpless upon the dirty floor. The boy's cry must have roused him. The lantern the British had left had guttered out but a stub of candle still burned. Benjy let himself down the hole.

"Suh . . ." he whispered anxiously.

Captain Lind moaned and pulled feebly against his ankle bonds. He had evidently struggled against the ropes to no avail and fallen into semi-consciousness. His arms were hideously swollen and at his wrists the dirt floor was stained with his blood. Benjy took one of the wooden trenchers and went out and filled it with water. He stripped off his wet hunting shirt and his tow linen undershirt. With the latter he washed the captain's bruised face. His lips were swollen and cut. He lay still for a long time. Benjy slopped water on both the captain's wrists and washed them gently. Then he went out to get more water. When he got back, the captain opened his eyes. Benjy gave him an end of his wet undershirt to suck.

"You . . ." the captain muttered weakly.

"Hush, I've to get you free and away for they will come back . . ." Benjy said.

"Let be, save your own skin, you idiot spawn of a coward," Lind said.

"Speak not so of my parent," Benjy said stoutly and childishly. "I did not betray you."

A string of most unpleasant epithets issued from the captain. Benjy thrust the sopping cloth back to his mouth.

"Hush, I say; revile me later," the boy said. He sought the bent tin cup and found it where it had been kicked in the corner. He twisted and worried it until he cracked an end and got a sharp edge to fray the cords that bound the captain's ankles. Lind's good leather boots had been some protection there.

The captain's wrists, however, were hideously torn. Benjy strained to cut the cords in the poor light of the single candle. He touched Lind's left arm after he had freed that wrist. Strong as Captain Lind was, he lapsed into unconsciousness under the pain. Taking the candle off the table, Benjy set it on the floor and carefully cut the sleeves of the captain's hunting shirt right up to his shoulders. Lind's arms were purpled from one end to the other. Suppose bones were broken. Benjy winced. He washed the captain's face again carefully until he opened his eyes once more.

"I've freed you," the boy announced. "Do you think you can get up and walk? Maybe I can push you up behind your shoulders. And hear me a moment," he astonished himself; he had never dreamed of speaking thus to Captain Lind but the situation demanded it, "I have the despatches from the ensign and I lost the British in Halfway Swamp. However, I have no horse and we must manage to get south along the river as far as possible before that patrol makes its way back here or those at the Westbury plantation return to reconnoiter. You must come, suh, as I say . . ."

Just then, as though to make him a liar in what he had just said, a long whinny came from outside. The boy jumped up and ran out. There stood the faithful Hamlet pawing the ground restlessly. Benjy, with no thought of danger though Hamlet was not generally friendly, threw both arms about the great black neck. The horse just tossed his head. Benjy ran in to convey the wonderful news to the captain. Pushing and prodding, Benjy got Lind into a semisitting position against the bedpost. The captain asked for more water and sucked it gratefully though the tin lip of the cup against his swollen mouth was a minor torment.

"I can't ride," he determined. He could not move either arm at all. And neither he nor the boy were in any position to determine how extensive a damage the big Irish corporal's boots had effected.

"You could lie across the saddle and I can walk Hamlet," Benjy proposed. "We'd better get started before dawn breaks."

The captain did not object to trying this. Benjy got him on his feet by bracing him behind his shoulder blades.

"You're soaking wet," Lind observed. It was the first quiet kindly thing he had said. He noticed something else but he did not mention it; the boy was stronger and a bit taller than he had thought him.

"I had to swim into the swamp to escape and later I swam down the creek aways," Benjy told him. "My hunting shirt's drying outside."

It wouldn't dry much in the cold November dampness, the captain thought. Thinking thus, he listened for a breeze and heard something else. "Hsst! Listen . . . I hear something."

Benjy's heart sank. This time they were helpless. He had the incriminating despatches beneath his belt. The British had quite thoroughly removed rifles, ax, hunting knife, even the captain's penknife. The slickery sneaky sound of stealthy approach was unmistakable. Benjy wanted to scream under the suspense. The captain leaned on the table, his hands and arms hanging useless. Hamlet whinnied. Then a low whistle broke out; the melody of *Sur le pont d'Avignon* floated on the air.

"God be praised, Antoine!" Captain Lind cried.

"You don't practice much security, friends!" Antoine cried. "Your horse loose on the doorstep?"

Benjy flew at him and thumped his shoulders in glee. But then they wasted not a moment. As Benjy told the whole story, Antoine got Lind out and lifted him into his saddle.

The captain bit his sore lips to avoid screaming from pain. Antoine ordered Benjy up on his horse Monsieur and he himself rode behind Hamlet's saddle on the animal's rump and held the captain erect safely and more comfortably than he would have been cross-saddle. They decided to try cutting cross-country between the Westbury and Guilliam plantations where the British would be least likely to look for them. Thus they could follow a creek spur to the Wenee-Black River where Lind's father had an upper country plantation rented to a tenant-farmer. Safely there, they could recover themselves. Antoine explained that his tardiness was due to the fact that he, too, had discovered that Cornwallis had sent the British Legion to look for Marion and had relayed the information to another scout who expected to be nearer to the brigade that night.

" 'Tis good you did thus," was Captain Lind's comment, for he could hardly expect in his present condition to get to his commander the next morning as they had originally planned.

The trip to the Lind place on the Black River was made without further difficulty. Examination of the captain's injuries, after Antoine had removed his clothes and bathed him, indicated no broken bones. The bruises would heal. In fact, by supper time of that day, Lind was already forcing himself to flex his fingers. Both officers were of one mind about attempting a return to Marion's position after dark. Benjy had hovered around all day, removed from the presence of Captain Lind, for his first clear words to Antoine after the latter's arrival had been: "Of all the bungling infants with whom I've been charged in this confounded war among women, children, and old men, this one is the worst. And home shall he go at first chance."

The time arrived, of course, when Benjy had to ask what

immediate disposition would be made of him. So he asked Antoine.

"You may ride M'sieu like last night and I'll ride with the captain," Antoine said.

"Get him a donkey instead and let him find his way home," snarled Lind and the boy's hurt feelings choked him painfully.

"Maladroitly or no, he saved the day and should have the right to report himself to the colonel," Antoine suggested gently.

"He has no sense of control, and now he's named me a masquerading spy from one end of Carolina to the other," David protested.

"I had to save your life! I saw no other way," Benjy protested.

"The devil of't, he speaks true," Antoine laughed.

"I'll save my own," the captain shouted. "This boy has no sense of when to speak or what to say."

Benjy recognized that that was true. He was most awfully confused and had ever been since the day of the burning September last.

"Perhaps not, but he did save your life, and from what he says, nor do you deny it, he also saved your hands in the nick of time from being crippled forever. Is that not something? Besides, my bonny captain, you be known through most of Carolina anyhow and by your right name and rank, amen," said Antoine.

"Let him go. I want him not, nor never did, muchly," the captain growled. But that put an end to it because he made no objection to Benjy mounting upon Monsieur when the time came.

CHAPTER SEVENTEEN

A Wild Ride

MARION's corps, augmented now to as large a contingent as he had had in months, was on the move when the scouts returned. Captain Lind was sent back with the rearguard under Major Horry, where he could ride in a wagon for a few days. Antoine and Benjy rode with the van, picked men who knew their way among the pine flats. Marion had not determined whether he would run from "Butcher" Tarleton or give battle. But it was the latter which he so much hoped to do. Therefore, he had scouts out in all directions. As they rode in, he sent others out. The swarthy little colonel, mounted on Ball, his favorite steed that he had taken from a defeated British colonel of that name, offered to receive Benjy alone when he heard the whole story of the adventure.

With his knees knocking, Benjy went to report to the commander at his lunch time. Marion was gnawing a chunk of hardtack like most of the men and drinking a mug of vinegared water.

"Here, boy, sit you down and dine with me. Seldom do you see such a magnificent repast," the colonel joked, offering another piece of the tough bread and a chunk of smoked ham and a hollowed branch with vinegar and water.

Benjy could have said that he had dined much more sumptuously at the tenant farmer's the day before, but he was smart enough to hold his tongue.

"Tell me now of your adventures and describe the kind of men who made up the British party," the colonel prompted.

Benjy sensed the man's even temper, deep sincerity, and eager interest. He found talking with him much easier than he had imagined it would be. Colonel Marion had a way with him, indeed; he made his subordinates comfortable though his manner was often severe. He was not so hard a man as Captain Lind nor yet so tenderhearted and friendly as Lieutenant DuMonseau.

"Sir," Benjy ventured at the end of his interview, "Captain Lind be angry wi' me and will not speak to me unless addressed and then not always. I do not understand why. I lied to save him, but he lied himself, at the beginning, until they discovered the horse with the things we had took from that ensign."

Marion nodded. "I don't think he has any compunction about you telling an untruth, nor should you have, yourself. A spy is a spy. The captain, boy, has not yet realized how well you did. I think you did remarkably well. But you gave him the impression that you were betraying him to save your skin and his. It is difficult, sometimes . . . often . . . to say where what is right and honorable or even wise and best, begins and ends. This is especially true in times like these we live in. Also, Benjamin, an angry man needs time to shake his temper down. Stay apart from the captain for a while. As a matter of fact, I intend to send Du-Monseau out tonight and you may go with him. I wish to call in ten men who promised to join me in case of a fight in this area, and I also want some information about Tarleton's approach. Drink your vinegar water, boy, keeps the fever away."

Benjy drank the sweet-sour sop as though it were an elixir of the gods, for he found the colonel's suggestions wonderfully encouraging. And he also liked being with the eager, merry Antoine.

Antoine and Benjy left at full dark when Colonel Marion set his brigade in motion again, moving stealthily and slowly back toward Jack's Creek and the neighborhood of General Richardson's plantation. The old general had recently died; his widow and children would certainly welcome Marion's troop. Yet little did Marion know that Tarleton's Legionnaires were coming in goodly numbers down the Santee Road to converge below Singleton's, where a Tory had informed them that "Mr. Marion might be found."

Antoine went up the Pocotaglio, crossed to the Black River, and came down along its east bank carrying his call to arms to the good Whigs of that neighborhood. Then he cut across the foothills of the Santee High Hills and came back down the Santee Road, watchful for British patrols but perhaps not as vigilant as he might have been. Antoine was by nature daring to the point of being reckless. Using a technique often employed by Marion's men, he rode off and on the road. And Benjy rode both before and behind the lieutenant, as it suited Antoine at the moment. They were both sober and gay. Much of the time Antoine sang his merry French folk songs. Benjy began to pick up some of the refrains: "planter les choux à la mode"; "font comme ça, comme çi"; "mon bon ami papillon, marie-toi donc."

Sometimes the boy got the man to talk about the siege of Charlestown and how he and Lind had ferried a dozen ablebodied men out to rouse the upper country. That was how they got involved with Colonel Buford in the bloody fracas at the Waxhaws. At lunch Antoine showed Benjy the long wound in his thigh, a livid scar now well healed. "An example of Tarleton's quarter, that . . . but in all truth, I cannot blame him personally except for lack of discipline. Now you might imagine, I suppose, a couple of companies belonging under our mutual friend Captain Lind disobeying an order because he happened to be dismounted during the fighting?"

Benjy laughed. "I'd like not to have to hold my ears when he called a muster the next day."

"So, you have said it, that's what I mean," Antoine replied. "Now you take me . . . I might, thoughtless, allow my men too much license, but not David Lind. But you see, he is and has been a company commander, and I doubt I shall ever be. I like my life too free and dangerous . . ." Even as he admitted this, he lolled in the saddle. And Benjy kicked his heels gaily and leaned over the pommel to pick a piece of fuzz out of one of Monsieur's eyelashes.

They were on the Trading Road. Both sides of it were thick with thorn and cane and gnarled vines. The air was surprisingly still and clear, no wind bore sound south to them. Not until the party of horsemen turned the last bend five hundred yards behind were man and boy alerted of pursuit. Antoine glanced back and muttered, "Dragoons!" as shouted commands behind broke the oncoming party of horsemen into a canter.

"Head down, hold tight," Antoine cried, "keep your legs quiet."

He struck Monsieur and dug in his heels but not before he had recognized the bright green jackets, black cuffs, and plumed helmets of the legionnaires.

An advancing rider shouted, "Halt up there! In the name of George Rex!"

Antoine dug in his spurs and at the same time talked encouragingly to his horse. "Give me wings, mon beau, give me wings." His face grew hot as he recognized that he had been unduly careless. "Keep your head in, Benjy, and down; they will shoot." He warned the boy who had to hold on with both hands and grip with his thighs besides.

"Around the next bend, let me down. I can hide," Benjy shouted above the din of the pounding hooves.

"Non! Non! Non! No time, and they'd see you before you could clear the roadside. Sit tight, be still."

The quick spurt of the big horse confirmed the suspicions of the British dragoon leader, for a thick voice shouted, "Take that fellow or bring him down!"

Benjy bent his head as far as he could and saw three dragoons break out in front of the rest, urging their mounts wildly; then three more did likewise. This Benjy reported to Antoine as well as the fact that two of the pursuers had evidently been ready for action for they raised horse pistols to fire. The horses of the British were probably no fresher at that time of day than Monsieur and certainly not as fine. But the cavalrymen did not spare their animals. They flogged the poor beasts furiously and began to gain. The road was caked and hard. The knotty brush had now given place to scrub fields, but Antoine had no time to see whether he stood a chance of leaving the road anywhere before the dragoons started firing. The balls whistled near, soon they would be within range. If Antoine swerved to turn to either side of the road, he would never clear the fire. Benjy reported that another set of six men were moving out in front. Antoine pulled out one of his horse pistols and handed it to the boy to examine the priming. Then, switching the reins for the gun, he turned, shot carefully and dropped a dragoon. But the others left the fellow to the main party behind and spurred madly on, not even giving him a look. Antoine could not take time to reload. Benjy could not reach the bullets.

Antoine cursed, as he had to slow down to avoid a farmer leading a cow. The British simply ran the fellow down on his knees and the cow into a ditch.

"Let me jump!" Benjy cried, "for I'm holding you back." This was true, he knew, and he supposed a boy who ran might have a better chance with the enemy than a man who did.

"Be still and hold tight," was all the lieutenant returned. But Benjy knew that Monsieur could never outrun all the pursuers with his double burden; they simply had to leave the road somewhere on the chance of cutting across country into woods or swamp where they had the possibility of escape.

"Watch for a cornfield, if I be right in memory of this stretch of the road," Antoine said a half mile farther on as the dragoons finished their next volley.

Horse pistols at best were clumsy weapons, short-ranged and inaccurate; but in a mounted pursuit they were useful if they happened to hit a part of their moving target. With a quick turn, risking a shot, Antoine could jump the low fieldstone wall of the cornfield, cross the stubble, and turn into the pine forest beyond. One man might try to follow him there but not a dozen. He could handle one. He urged Monsieur to a final spurt, seeking to get far enough out of range to risk the jump.

"We'll take the wee stone wall and away to the woods, M'sieu'," he said fondly to the horse. "Vite! vite! we must not let the green devils know what we're up to. Marion needs the news of the legion here. Now then . . . Benjy, bear to the left and keep your head down."

Antoine pulled the right rein sharply. Monsieur turned and prepared for the short sharp jump. The dragoons gained several paces. The foremost rider had clear firing. He had prepared his weapon; he took fairly careful aim and shot. The others had wasted ammunition all the way down; this shot was successful. It got Antoine in the upper part of his right thigh. He felt the sting and reeled toward it. Checking the horse, he drew him back to the road.

"If you swing me up now, I'll fall out, M'sieu' . . . curses, he must have broken a bone, confound him! Always my poor thighs . . ."

He laid on the whip that he so seldom used. They rode on in a frantic burst of speed. Benjy felt his cheeks burn and his eyes sting with the force of the wild ride. But Monsieur could not keep up such a pace. He was exhausted. He gasped heavily and his coat reeked with foam and sweat. Behind a dragoon dropped off to shoot his finished beast.

"Farm or plantation house ahead left," Benjy managed to gasp. "Road ahead . . ."

Antoine struck into the narrow overgrown path, suppose the house were empty? Oh, well, it was shelter, respite, and he could go no more. He was slipping badly for he had no holding power in his numb right leg. As soon as he could see the house, he gave Benjy the reins and grasped the pommel himself with both hands, sheltering the boy between his arms.

"Take him . . . across . . ." Antoine muttered then.

And Benjy did guide the horse on a shorter course, a diagonal across what had once been a well-kept lawn. At the front door of the house Benjy jumped off the horse and ran up two steps to hammer with both fists. Antoine half fell off the spent horse that stood gasping, blood flecking from his nostrils.

"Gi' me your hand . . . and then open the door and go in," Antoine whispered.

The British dragoons were already in the overgrown

driveway. Two tore recklessly across the lawn tearing it up still more. Benjy pushed the door in and dragged Antoine across the threshold. His doeskin breeches were covered with blood. He pulled himself across the small hall to a stair that led to the second storey. There he turned to meet both the enemy and the mistress of the house who had come from the kitchen at the commotion.

"I'm sorry," Antoine gasped, propping himself against the post of the staircase by wrapping an arm about it. "I've been shot . . . British patrol . . . take care of the boy!" He spoke as if the whole business were an everyday occurrence. "Keep your servants away," he added.

"I'll get my husband," the good woman said, as she heard the dragoons outside.

The next moment, someone flung the door open again.

CHAPTER EIGHTEEN

A Touch of Tarleton's Dragooning

THE BRIGHT green coats of the legionnaires made splotches of color against the white woodwork of the hall. Antoine must have felt dizzy and weak because he jammed his right fist hard over the wound in his thigh and looked up to meet the beady dark eyes of a stocky Legion sergeant. Benjy hung within the edge of the staircase side as motionless as though he were part of it. The sergeant swaggered into the middle of the hall with his pistol leveled. He was brawny and bullish like the one who had questioned Captain Lind. Six or eight dragoons swarmed behind him blocking the doorway.

"What business made you run so lively from a party as large as ours?" the sergeant demanded, glaring at Antoine.

The young man was silent. Benjy barely breathed.

"Be you one of that Marion's men, eh?" the sergeant asked. "Sure and they run that quick when they see us coming, heh, men?" he continued contemptuously to his fellows, who laughed.

Antoine swayed forward and put out his left hand to steady himself; he was pale as fog, nerves shuddered in his good leg. He must have been light-headed, too, Benjy thought for he cried out too recklessly, "A man be not free to ride or run as he chooses?"

Benjy bit his lip and wished Antoine had done likewise.

145

The burly sergeant grinned. "Ye stop for the king's horsemen or we make ye, eh, boys?" He elbowed a man behind who roared, "Aye!"

Antoine frowned as though he only partially knew what was going on. The sergeant swung his pistol flourishingly. "What were you doing on the road, man, say?" Each word came on the same pitch, dully, threateningly.

After shaking his head as if to clear his understanding, Antoine replied with his natural impudence, "I rode, you idiot, as you saw!"

"Hold your lip. I'll take none of't. You tell me what you know respectfully, I've a pistol on you. Have you any papers?"

"No, and nothing to tell. I've had a scratch from your pistol, you see." He moved his hand upon the bloody thigh.

"Search him," the sergeant commanded a dragoon.

The fellow came to Antoine's side. With a quick movement, he doubled up his bloody fist. Hurt as he was, he knocked the legionnaire across the hall into the arms of one of his fellows.

"I said I have no papers. I don't lie," Antoine shouted.

The sergeant's finger flickered on the trigger. Tarleton could depend on him to be inhuman when he was riled. A slow hush spread over the circle of troopers.

"I can think of some questions I'd like answered regarding your skulking Mr. Marion who has cut down enough of our express riders and made off with enough of our supply wagons. I'll give you three minutes; you either talk or die!" and he added a string of curses. Then he took a big silver watch from his jacket pocket, studied its face ostentatiously, and handed it to the nearest soldier. "Three minutes to make up your mind, sirrah!"

Antoine pushed his left shoulder back hard against the

newel post of the stair and waited. A little sneer turned down the corners of his mouth. His unpowdered black curls were damp and tumbled on his forehead. His lustrous black eyes smoldered. But loss of blood already gave him a pallor. The seconds passed. A small puddle of blood gathered on the carpeting of the first stair step.

"Stand where ye be!" the sergeant shouted suddenly.

Antoine started and Benjy jumped at the unexpected exclamation. A dragoon leveled another horse pistol toward the passageway. The farmer's wife had returned with her husband. They stood obediently some paces behind Benjy, still in their tracks as they had been bidden. Antoine flashed a quick glance from the sergeant to the couple.

"Have done! I do not know these people and I like not to mess up their house. I have heard of your Colonel Tarleton's penchant for this type of amusement. If you would not have me your prisoner as I am, if murder be a game with you, sergeant," he was bold, indeed, too bold, Benjy knew, "your move!"

The sergeant looked toward the woman. He paused another moment, perhaps one beyond the three he had called. "Mark that I give you fair chance to talk," he announced grimly.

The gathered dragoons watched Antoine curiously, wondering if his insolence were bravado or genuine daring. He showed no fear. It seemed almost as though fear had been left out of his make-up. Benjy's throat closed tight; surely, the sergeant merely threatened and would not shoot the young man again, in cold blood. Why didn't Antoine say something, anything to gain respite?

The sergeant spoke once more. "Have you naught to say? I now offer you the liberal terms of allegiance that the Earl Cornwallis allowed the citizens of Charlestown after

147

the siege, in gracious similitude of the kindliness of His Sovereign Majesty." He had practiced that speech on others; it ran out of his mouth smoothly enough.

Antoine's black eyes blazed. "A curse upon His Sovereign Majesty!" he shouted. "May he be . . ."

The sergeant pulled the trigger of his horse pistol as he drew breath. An intense silence seemed to hang suspended after the ring of the shot. Antoine caught at his side with both hands and reeled forward to the floor. Benjy clapped his hands over his face, but the farmer's wife with a muffled cry ran to the stricken young man. The dragoons did not stop her.

Then commotion and clamor filled the doorway with more dragoons. A sharp, thick voice filtered through. "Confound you all! Out of my way! What the devil's to do here?" A riding whip slashed viciously against the buck-skinned thighs of the regulars who had jammed the doorway. The dragoons parted, leaving a path for the commander who strode in abruptly. The sergeant, pistol still smoking, turned to face him. Antoine stirred, and the plantation housewife lifted his head into her lap.

"Chelsea, what goes on?" Lieutenant Colonel Tarleton demanded. Benjy stared at the renowned Legion commander. He was shorter than Antoine and not much older, certainly younger than Captain Lind, a stocky man with dark skin, piercing black eyes, unpowdered chestnut hair showing beneath his fancy plumed helmet. Benjy had not exactly imagined him thus. "Well?" Tarleton roared with impatience.

"I shot him," Sergeant Chelsea nodded at Antoine calmly. "I could get nothing out of him save profanity against the king, sir."

"Helpful that is," Tarleton exclaimed callously. He came

to look at Antoine closely, then asked softly, "Did you shoot to kill?"

"He should live a while," Chelsea replied very low and with a significant twist of his lip.

"Send in Mr. Stapleton," the colonel ordered and the surgeon, a tall thin middle-aged man, came immediately. "Have a look here, sir, then I will talk with the fellow," Tarleton ordered. He unbuckled his heavy saber belt and tossed it on a chair in the nearby sitting room. Then he removed his helmet and brushed a hand through his hair. Suddenly he whirled upon Benjy, who still stood like a statue beside the staircase. "Who are you?"

Before the boy could think of what to say, the woman of the house interpolated. "He be my nephew, and I'm Frances Reed . . ." she looked piercingly at her husband, a thickset man who trembled at her boldness.

"Mind your manners and what you say, I be authorized to punish rebels wi' fire and the sword," the colonel said; Benjy knew he was suspicious.

"I see that," Mistress Reed returned sturdily. "I be neither friend nor foe . . . use my house, but pray, sir, gi' leave to couch this poor man so ill-used by your sergeant?" Her courage was impressive.

"Ill-used?" Colonel Tarleton raised his thick eyebrows. "He ran from my men on the road, my sergeant knows what to do wi' that kind. If you liked not his treatment, let it be a warning to you and your family," he slurred the latter word and looked keenly at Benjy, "and your servants."

Sergeant Chelsea nodded toward Benjy. "Might I have a word wi' the colonel about that boy, sir?" he wagged his head significantly.

"Later. Get that rebel where 'twill be more comfortable for me to question him." Tarleton wiped some of Antoine's blood fastidiously off his boot onto Mistress Reed's passageway carpeting.

The surgeon ordered a couple of dragoons to carry Antoine upstairs, but the young man protested toward Mistress Reed. "In mercy, madam, let me die on the ground floor near the out-of-doors, couch me by a window."

Benjy wanted to shriek "Don't die," but he remembered in time that he was now supposed to be a stranger to Antoine. He did not think he could pose indifferent long.

Mistress Reed led the way, then, into the sitting room and had a servant fix a bed on a low couch. Pillows and comforters made Antoine's head even with the window edge. Benjy hovered nearby, asked if he could open the mullioned window and shutters. The surgeon denied him. After examining both wounds, the doctor sent for Tarleton, who had been making himself free in the kitchen and ordering supper for his entire party.

"Chelsea shot this fellow twice, once on the road," Mr. Stapleton told the colonel. Benjy listened from a corner in the hall. "I can take the first ball out but it would be useless work and agony for him."

"He'll die, of course?"

"Surely, in a day or so . . . you know the kind of wound. His youth and strength be no help. Did Chelsea think he had information that suffering might make him divulge?"

Tarleton shrugged. "Maybe . . . he was brashly defiant, I have heard. Does he know he will die?"

"I can't say," the surgeon answered.

"There's no point in telling him," Tarleton said. "Take the one bullet out, perhaps he'll talk . . . and I shall be handy to listen . . ." He could not have meant to be kind. Benjy shivered.

Mr. Stapleton returned to where Antoine lay looking at the figured wallpaper above a cabinet near his feet. Benjy slipped from the corner of the hall through the open door into a corner of the sitting room. The surgeon turned to his mate, a lad of about nineteen. "We can take the bullet in the thigh out," he began.

"Do you suggest thus to cure me, sir?" Antoine asked bitterly.

The surgeon swallowed uncomfortably.

"I know just how this last wound will work, Mister, why should I go through the small hell of probing? Tie me up; when I lie quiet, the pain's not bad," Antoine covered his eyes with a hot arm.

"I'll make you as easy as I can," Stapleton said. Then he noticed Benjy gawking at him and sent him out. And the boy bolted headlong into Colonel Tarleton, who caught his shoulder in a fierce grip and cuffed him hard enough to make him gasp.

"Can you speak for our prisoner, boy, that you hang about him?"

Benjy murmured, "No, suh," meekly.

"Then off with you!" the colonel pinched his ear between his thumb and forefinger nails until it bled and tears started to Benjy's eyes.

Miserable, the boy fled to the kitchen and made himself useful about the table Mistress Reed was fixing for the British colonel and his officers: a major, two captains, four lieutenants, the surgeon and his mate. After these men had dined, the Reeds set up planks out-of-doors for the soldiery who made short and noisy shrift of stew, pudding, several gallons of sweet cider, and a cache of ripe pippins.

Later, Colonel Tarleton spread some maps out on the big kitchen table. Benjy managed to get a look at one. It was a remarkably good map of that area; a Tory militia officer in buckskins did an excellent job of interpreting it for the colonel.

"We'll to General Richardson's place in the morning, then, since this slippery old fox has fled the dugout at Singleton's," Tarleton remarked. "I've never seen a man skip so dexterously in and out and through the confounded swamps with which this horrid country is pocked."

Benjy would have liked to have run off immediately with this news and warned Colonel Marion, but he could not leave Antoine. He was genuinely upset. His only comfort lay in the fact that he supposed he could never get away without being caught. He sat bundled in the chimney corner of the kitchen, not wanting to attract Tarleton's attention. But Sergeant Chelsea came in and spotted him.

"A word wi' ye, Colonel, about that boy," the formidable sergeant pointed a fat finger. "He lies to say he are of this place because he were riding wi' the prisoner . . . I saw him get down at the house front!"

Benjy felt his color fade and then rise to give him away. The cavalry commander looked at him searchingly as though he could read right into his mind. Then he beckoned to him. Benjy came before him, anticipating another cuff. "So . . ." Tarleton said, then added, "Now bully for you, Chelsea, why'n't you shoot him for a rebel, too?"

Benjy shuddered. The young colonel laughed; he may have meant his words lightly but Benjy was afraid of his life with the brutish sergeant.

"Are you a rebel, boy, eh?" Tarleton asked.

Benjy looked up into his black eyes. He could not judge what he saw in them. He remembered the puncturing nails and it was all he could do not to touch his ear protectingly.

"Speak!"

Benjy shook his head to indicate he would not. Tarleton gripped his shoulder again and spun him before him. "Come, we'll see your friend and he may have something to say, heh?" Propelled into the sitting room, Benjy felt his throat tighten with fear. The room was dark and still; was Antoine asleep?

Tarleton lit a tall candelabrum from a taper in the hall sconce. He, too, may have supposed Antoine to be asleep. Moving the light close to the couch, the young cavalry leader stood a moment looking down at the wounded man. Antoine breathed evenly but with effort. His face was paper white. Dark circles lay like purple shadows beneath his closed eyes. Otherwise he appeared strong, brawny, handsome. He had a refined strength rather than mere height and weight. And what a breadth of shoulder . . . and he was young. Quite suddenly, the heavy eyelids lifted and the dark eyes reached up toward Tarleton's equally dark and penetrating ones.

"Not sleeping?" the Briton asked.

"I can't," Antoine flung a hot restless arm across his forehead. "You weren't watching for me to die, Colonel?" he asked with sudden acidity.

"Hardly," Tarleton twisted his full mouth, "I'd not cheat me of our conversation . . . stand quiet, boy!" he ground his fingers into Benjy's shoulder though the boy had certainly not attempted to move. "You look familiar," Tarleton went on to Antoine. "I rarely forget a face; who are you?" He unbuttoned his jacket as though the room were too warm though it was comfortable.

Antoine looked at him firmly. "If you know me, you have a superlative memory," he smiled painfully.

"A poor memory is a deficiency in a soldier," Tarleton snapped. "Yet I cannot remember where I have seen you."

Pushing his hand upon his hip to give him leverage against his pain, Antoine pulled himself up on his pillows. "I was at the Waxhaws, Colonel Tarleton, a lieutenant under Colonel Buford. My name is Antoine DuMonseau. I doubt we exchanged blows but I was in the heat of the fray and wounded. You may have seen my face."

"So you are now wi' Marion?"

"It was your sergeant who suggested this," Antoine shrugged. "Should I have admitted being with Marion to have died easier . . . Chelsea meant for me to die slowly. I understand just how, do you?"

Tarleton met his eyes again but somewhat against his will, it seemed. Benjy stirred against the biting pain of Tarleton's grip. The colonel released him with another cuff that made him gasp.

"Let the boy be, I shall suffer enough for both of us!" Antoine cried. "It's a cunning way to shoot a man and I know a saber cut that's quite as neat and so must you," he flushed in sudden anger. "I can't lie here like this." He struggled to lift himself but soon fell back among the pillows choking. "Why couldn't he have made a clean job of it?"

Benjy stood at the bottom of the bed with his fists knotted. Something in Antoine's white emotion probed beneath Tarleton's military hauteur and personal arrogance for a moment.

"I would hope I should have, you deserved it," he said.

"I've always supposed I could die with courage, even hang with courage if I had the misfortune to be caught in the wrong situation, but instead I must waste away slowly . . . I'm a coward about this, I guess . . ."

Benjy wanted to deny it. The colonel said, half callously, "Too bad you know, even the surgeon is cruel, I suppose . . . You're no coward."

Antoine reached out his hand and touched the colonel's knee. "Not so much a one as to inform you, at least," he said with a flash of his natural boldness. "I saw a fellow die like this at camp and 'twould have been kinder if someone had had nerve enough to put another bullet in his heart. But having got it out, I feel better. I couldn't ask my best friend or my worst enemy to put me out of it, could I? And you, sir, are neither."

"Blast Chelsea!" Tarleton exclaimed. "How old are you?"

Antoine fetched a thin smile. "Twenty-two, do they not say the good die young?"

The stocky cavalry commander coughed drily.

"You're young yourself; until I saw you this close by, I'd thought of you as rather different," Antoine admitted; Benjy nodded in his corner at the end of the bed.

"Butcher Tarleton! My unsavory reputation?" He curled a scornful lip. "I'm twenty-six but I've not felt so young for a year."

"That's because you've been the lion of the hour," Antoine said wisely. "Success matures one early. Failure would leave you very young again."

Tarleton chewed his lip thoughtfully.

Antoine broke the silence as if it weighed heavily upon him. "If Chelsea expects me to talk when I've suffered enough, he's wasting his time . . . and yours, Colonel . . ." He took a deep breath and pain twisted his face; he grasped at the couch edge. "Besides, I know enough not to try to eat . . ."

"Stop!" Tarleton backed a step and overturned a chair in his way. " 'Tis not my affair to watch you die. Be about it in your own good time."

Benjy gulped.

"Wait you one moment, Colonel Tarleton," Antoine

pulled in another painful breath. "The boy who shrinks from both of us in the corner there, he was with me and is naught to the woman of the house. Hold the lie against neither of us and let him go . . . and gi' him my horse."

"You be bold in your way, dying!" Tarleton half sneered but then added, "I like a bold fellow. Come here, boy." Benjy approached, his knees shaking. "Shall I believe your Colonel Marion enlists the services of children like this?" Tarleton looked at Benjy so carefully that the boy rather expected him to ask him to open his mouth so he could count his teeth.

Antoine, after a spasm of pain, smiled gently. "Remember that I never admitted an acquaintance with Marion."

"So you didn't, knowing withal that I would put him down an' it took every ounce of my strength. I be under no compulsion to grant you a request, rebel," Tarleton puckered his full lips. "I leave you with the boy and warn him there be limits to my indulgence and my sergeant gives none!"

He strode off. Benjy sat down beside Antoine but they didn't say much at all. At nine o'clock Mistress Reed came to show the boy to a trundle bed in her own chamber.

CHAPTER NINETEEN

Shadow and Sunshine

FOR A LONG time Benjy could not sleep. Mistress Reed went up and down, watching over Antoine. Also, Benjy kept berating himself because he had not paid closer attention to Colonel Tarleton's staff officers and the maps in the kitchen. He had managed to whisper to Antoine about the plan to go to General Richardson's. Antoine had told him that when the moment came, perhaps not until the British left but shortly thereafter, he must go and seek Colonel Marion and tell him all he had heard. Thus Benjy had realized that he might have listened more carefully. Of course, Antoine had warned him several times to do nothing rash and bold, not to sneak behind doors or listen noticeably but to be quite open and forthright so he would not be suspect.

At dawn, the soldiery rose with the blowing of a bugle. Benjy felt as though he had never been asleep. He heard the troops go off to water, dress down and feed their horses, and possibly, the boy thought, to prepare for a march. He hoped so.

Immediately after a breakfast of bacon, eggs, and hot bread, Colonel Tarleton gathered his staff together for briefing. Only the surgeon and his mate, Gray, went in to see Antoine. He seemed much weaker and could hardly speak. He asked to have the window opened at his side so he could see the sunrise.

Mr. Stapleton put a fresh dressing on Antoine's thigh but he did not touch the other wound. He shook his head gently and significantly to Benjy. The boy knew that the lieutenant was failing; his throat clogged. After the doctor and his assistant left, Antoine turned toward the open air. It was a fresh dewy morning with a tinge of frost.

"I would it were spring," Antoine whispered so low that Benjy had to ask him to say it again. "I would it were spring with the trees burgeoning. Well, a man may not pick his time. Benjy, notice the number of men if you have a chance, and particularly seek mention or sight of field pieces, cannon, you hear?" Saying all this was difficult for Antoine; he had to space each word painstakingly. He breathed more quickly than usual and seemed to be in considerable pain. "Benjy . . ." before he could say more a big brown muzzle came over the window edge and nudged for Antoine's hand on the coverlet. "Ah, M'sieu', mon beau cheval . . ." the sick man whispered and stroked the soft lips and velvet nose. "They've not penned you in, thank heaven! Benjy . . ."

"Yes, suh," the boy knelt beside him to be close.

"Hear me . . . take . . . M'sieu' to . . . you know . . ." Benjy nodded and mouthed "to Colonel Marion" because a dragoon walked sentry duty in the hall outside the sitting room door and for all they knew another marched outside the window. Monsieur whinnied and snorted. Antoine soothed him but his hand trembled. "Benjy . . . good boy . . ." his voice kept trailing away between words feebly . . . "hear . . . look . . . seek . . . saddle . . . give to . . . promise . . . give to . . . Marion only . . ."

Benjy promised, thinking hard on each word, praying not to forget any, not at all sure of any complete meaning from the whole. He hoped somehow that Antoine would

be able to explain more carefully. But by the time the
Legion bugler had tossed off his first call to "Boots and Saddles," Benjy knew. And a moment or two after the handsome young man had closed his eyes, Mistress Reed heard
the boy sobbing. She came into the sitting room and coaxed
Monsieur's head outside the ledge and closed the shutters.
The shadow of death fell across the couch.

"Come," the good woman lifted Benjy by his arms, "that
British commander would speak with you. You'd better go
to him. I will do all that I can do for your young friend."

In the hall Colonel Tarleton, booted and spurred, jack-
eted and caped, and with his fearful saber at his side, was
pulling on his riding gloves. The black plumes on his helmet waved in the morning breeze, for the front door stood
ajar. He glared upon Benjy. "Is he dead?" he asked harshly.

The boy said, "Yes, suh," thickly but firmly.

"No tears?" The colonel glowered upon the boy as
though he would promote them.

Benjy tightened, ground his teeth together, and murmured yet firmly, "You need not weep for the brave!"

"Say you so?" the cavalryman lifted an eyebrow
quizzically but the boy's steadfastness must have touched
him. "You be worthy of your friend, I take it," he flung
open the door. "Against luck in my search for that foxy
Marion, I honor his last request and do you rest from the
performance of any mischief, ye hear? My patrols be
everywhere about." Benjy strained to understand the Lan-
castrian accent. "Soldier, bring me the beast," Tarleton
shouted to a dragoon. The fellow came before the house
steps leading Monsieur. "Is that your lieutenant's horse?"
Benjy nodded. "Sink me! what a handsome beast, lead him
away before I change my mind!"

"Yes, suh," Benjy went out into the blaze of full sun-

shine and took the bridle from the soldier. He hid his face
on Monsieur's soft brown cheek and a couple of soldiers
laughed.

Colonel Tarleton transfixed them with a glance and an
oath and vaulted into his own saddle. Raising his right
hand, the young colonel shouted to his bugler, "Sound
march!" With a jingling, jangling commotion the troops
came out from every angle and direction about the big
farmhouse, breaking neatly into road formation.

Two small cannon, the type commonly called grasshop-
pers, were brought up in the rear of the cavalcade; and
some foot soldiers, garbed in the scarlet and buff of British
regulars, walked behind a wagon with supplies. Benjy supposed they were engineers. He also overheard, and tucked
carefully away in his mind, a report to the commander that
carried clearly on the east wind: "Sir, an express from the
other companies has just arrived and indicates that we shall
join by ten o'clock."

As soon as all sight and sound of the departing enemy
was gone, Benjy studied Antoine's saddle, remembering
what the dying lieutenant had whispered so piecemeal:
"look . . . seek . . . saddle . . . and give to . . . promise . . . give to . . . Marion only . . ." What could the
cryptic sentence mean? For all the boy could see it was an
ordinary saddle, thick and sturdy, of good leather, cut in
the English cavalry style, but in no way extraordinary. Carefully, Benjy searched its side pockets but only one contained
anything: some gun patches, a bit of flint and steel, some
scraps of foolscap frayed at the edges and with nothing
written upon them, a roll of linen; that was all. The boy in-
spected underneath, too, and shook out the fold of blanket
while Monsieur tossed his head in the bright morning sunshine. Satisfied that there was nothing, Benjy examined the

saddlebags next. The British soldiers had removed Antoine's two horse pistols and all his ammunition. Benjy supposed that the colonel would not trust him with arms of any kind. Mistress Reed's husband, too, had been forced to reveal all of his firearms and supplies. The saddlebags did contain a few things, several sacks of cornmeal and hominy, a slab of bacon, a leather pouch to serve as an extra canteen, ends of saddle straps, a farrier's needle, sinew for mending. These the British had not removed. Benjy supposed there had never been any money, personal items, or papers. Marion's men, especially his scouts, traveled as lightly as possible in case of unexpected capture.

Mistress Reed made the boy eat a hearty breakfast though he was not much for it, thinking constantly of the quiet form in her sitting room. She also packed him a lunch of pone and dried beef. By nine of the grandfather clock in her hall, he was on his way. As the big horse bore him smoothly along, he considered how happy Colonel Marion would be to receive such an animal. Except for Captain Lind's Hamlet, Benjy had never seen a handsomer horse. To which of his senior officers would the little colonel give Monsieur, since his own light-footed, smaller Ball suited his short stature so well? Benjy thought all these things and tried to blot out the bitter memories of Antoine. But when the distress of his death intruded, the boy could only believe sadly that recklessness, and recklessness alone, had promoted Antoine's fate.

Carefully, as he had learned in his association with the captain and the lieutenant, Benjy made his way along the swamp edges and at the side of the road. Twice he had to hide from British patrols. Once he was within breath's hearing of two buckskin-legginged, breech-clouted provincials, evidently posted off from Tarleton's main body. These fellows were bribing a farmer's son with a half-crown piece to spread the word that Tarleton, disgusted with the treacherous hide-and-seek of Mister Marion, was heading back to Camden.

This bit of information Benjy was certain was false. Tarleton was shrewd, too, almost as foxy as his opponent. Benjy kicked Monsieur lightly on the next lap of his journey, for time was precious. For one thing, Colonel Marion had to be warned that the British now knew his approximate position; a servant had told Tarleton just before his departure about an American party at Jack's Creek. This, Benjy knew, coincided with the information Antoine had told upon his arrival at the old mill.

The big horse carried the lithe boy like a feather. By dusk, when he stopped to ask for a drink at a farmer's well and sat down to eat his jerky and pone, he was within hail of his destination. Arriving at full dark, he was astonished to find that Marion had left the encampment. It was plain to see that he had been there with a large body of reinforcements. But where was he now? A patriot landowner told Benjy that he understood "the Americans went out after some patrols of British soldiers that the good colonel had got wind of." Benjy's heart began to pound. Suppose Colonel Marion had believed Tarleton's whole brigade, augmented by Harrison's provincials, to be nothing more than a few patrols?

Swallowing his last mouthful of food as he mounted, the boy set off in the direction the man indicated. In a way it was droll that the British were coming down to post at Richardson's and Marion was sneaking up to the same place from the south. And yet would Colonel Marion steal into an ambush? Benjy slapped Monsieur's neck with the reins and coaxed him faster as they sped along the creek path.

Suddenly, a holler startled them; then two shadowy figures blocked the road. One reached up and caught Monsieur's bridle; the other poised a long rifle.

"Alack! no loyalist spy this, 'tis Lind's boy," cried a familiar voice. It was William, the youngest of the James boys, who was not much Benjy's senior himself and was acting rear outpost.

Within a few minutes Benjy had made known enough of his story to be taken directly to Colonel Marion.

"You say he has two fieldpieces? You're sure? I've sent scouts to check those campfire flickerings at General Richardson's. Stand ready to move in either direction!" the colonel ordered.

The word went down the lines. Benjy was amazed at the number of horsemen. Four hundred they had amassed in the last week. While this seemed a lot, Benjy believed that Tarleton had at least twelve hundred if all the companies that were to have joined him had arrived on time. Marion shook his head at this information and frowned.

"I know not what to do, for I would destroy what I can of the enemy, believe me," he muttered to Major Horry. "Send for Captain Lind," he added.

The captain came immediately. He seemed to have full use of his right arm again but he carried the left slung still in a cavalry strap.

"The boy has ill news," the colonel told him with no preliminaries. "The lieutenant is dead, murdered in cold blood by one of Tarleton's sergeants. Would you go? It happened at the Reed place on Black Creek. The boy can say exactly how to get to't."

They stood looking steadily at each other in the dull light of a torch that a trooper held, the colonel and the captain. Their mutual grief choked them. Benjy, watching, could not keep back hot tears that soon overflowed.

Captain Lind turned to him with a set face. He spoke thickly. "Did you serve him as you did me?" he asked.

Benjy broke into sobs and grasped Monsieur's long mane with both hands. He did not know exactly what the captain meant; but the words, in the tone they were said, hurt him.

"Let be, Captain Lind," Colonel Marion cried. "The boy loved Lieutenant DuMonseau."

"So did I . . . love him," the captain said. "Come apart here with me, Benjy, and tell me the story . . ."

"Not now!" the colonel interposed. "Time is too urgent. Go to Reed's if you would, Captain, and see the Lieutenant decently buried. You have my leave. Then seek us in that same area, for should I retreat, 'tis there I would go, setting the swamps between."

"Yes, sir," the captain said. Without a word of comfort to the weeping boy, he put foot to stirrup and veered Hamlet around. But his courtesy farewell to the colonel was gruff, thick with his own hurt. Benjy supposed that in the dim quiet of the lonely road, the stern captain, too, wept for his friend.

CHAPTER TWENTY

Of Pride and Shame

In the next hour excitement mounted. First the brigade crept cautiously toward the Richardson plantation. The lights from the British campfires grew brighter. The rear guard caught some Tories sneaking in the bushes. One lied about Tarleton's numbers but admitted that there were dragoons at the Richardson place. Marion couldn't decide whether or not to attack. He sent for Benjy again.

"You are sure about the cannon?" the little Huguenot asked again and again.

The boy insisted but he was frightened. He missed Antoine; he even missed the stern strength of Captain Lind. Just then, across a low hedge, a man called out. A moment later, one of the guards reported to the colonel. The fellow was the son of General Richardson, a paroled Continental officer who claimed to know Marion well.

The colonel went up to the hedge himself to speak with the young man, who warned Marion to stay at a distance because he thought his breath was yet contagious with the smallpox from which he had just recovered. Everything young Richardson said corroborated what Benjy had reported. The entire British Legion was in force and under arms, lying in ambush.

Colonel Marion came back and patted Benjy on the head, leaning down from Ball. Then with calm good humor, he ordered a right-about-face of his entire force. Leading the van himself with Major Horry, he set off in a rapid march around the Woodyard Swamp. Unfortunately, the rearguard let one of the recently captured Tories escape in the confusion of the turn-about. The fellow must have run directly to Tarleton because, before long, the rearguard reported that the British were in full pursuit.

By this time Marion had ridden his corps across Richbour's mill dam. Feeling relatively safe, he called a halt for breakfast. However, they had a very short one; upon confirmation of the British advance, the colonel jumped upon Ball and led the way through the great pine barrens toward the head of the Pocotaglio River down which he rode full speed till the horses were foaming. Benjy rode behind Captain Milton, who had been lent Monsieur in order to give his own horse to an unmounted sergeant. From sunrise they rode, with the British Legion occasionally within sight behind them. What a mad chase it was, through the pine woods and over the swampy places, some of them the lowest in the whole colony. When they could use a road, they kicked the dust up until it choked them, and often enough they tracked across just-harvested fields or trampled down cornstalks.

At mid-afternoon Colonel Marion ordered a crossing at Benbow's Ferry. The water of the ford was icy cold, but the men laughed to put it between them and Tarleton. For the past hour no green horsemen had been seen, but Marion was not convinced he had escaped. He planned for the arrival of the British. He sent his best riflemen under McCottry to form a reception committee on the western side of the river while handpicked men felled trees in the narrow path that led down the bluff to the ferry slip. Marion then told his officers that if Tarleton made it across the river, the brigade was to scatter and escape and then come together again and make successive small stands at the passes through Pudding, Clap, and Flat swamps. The final point of rendezvous, if they were successful in defeating or shaking the enemy, was to be Kingstree.

Having made his plans, the colonel sat down to wait. Nothing happened. Eventually, the entire brigade rested easier. After all, they had the turbulent water of the Black River between them and danger. About midnight, a scout came in with the welcome news that Tarleton had turned his weary dragoons back at Ox Swamp.

Just after dawn, Captain Lind rode in with more news. Tarleton had not simply returned whence he had come. He had laid waste General Richardson's plantation, dug up the General's recently buried corpse, destroyed all the crops and livestock, and then in his most vengeful mood raided and robbed, devastated and burned a great width of country from Nelson's Ferry to Camden, including the mills that belonged to General Sumpter.

Benjy, listening to all this from the gnarled roots of a big tree, knew that he could be grateful he had met with the young British cavalryman before Colonel Marion had eluded him . . . or the Reeds might not have had their house over their heads. Thinking this, the boy remembered Monsieur and the saddle. Seeking the horse, where Captain Milton had tethered him, he then asked permission to speak to the commander. But the colonel was breakfasting in the gray dawn and mending his ragged uniform jacket with the help of his servant Oscar.

Captain Lind sought the boy and sat down beside him. "Mistress Reed told me something of your adventures," he said. He seemed in a gentler mood than usual. "Is't true that Antoine defied the sergeant?"

Benjy nodded.

"He was ever a hothead, and hasty," David muttered. "I take it his defiance did him small good."

"It got him killed, when he could have lied," Benjy whispered. "He could have sworn for King George and had that Legion surgeon to treat the wound in his leg!"

"No!" the captain fairly roared to rattle the dried leaves on the trees. "This you never understand, boy. He could have lied before, yes, to save his skin and escape, or to prevent anyone from offering him the oath, but were they to offer me the oath or the major there or the colonel himself, I doubt not we'd all die than take it falsely. Don't you really see that, boy?"

Benjy stood clenching his fists as his confusion confounded him again. "No, no! I don't see; I know only that Antoine be dead and I loved him!" He burst into a passion of tears.

The captain listened for a moment or two and then hauled back his right palm and slapped him. Benjy stifled his sobs. Captain Lind walked round and round a big tree flexing his left arm and rubbing its yet sore places with his right fingers. When the boy's tears were dried, the captain came behind him and put his hand on his shoulder.

"Hear me now, don't you suppose I wept for him, too?" he asked.

Benjy was nothing if not outspoken and honest. "You seem rather to blame him and me both for his death," he stated.

"We stand at odds, then, boy?" the captain asked, a little bitterly.

"Yes, suh, ever thus," Benjy returned.

Captain Lind turned on his bootheel and strode away. Benjy knew then that he would be denied the story of Antoine's burial. It was his own fault; he controlled his feelings well from that moment.

During the hour, Gabriel Marion, the colonel's tall nephew, came to take Benjy to the commander. Grasping Monsieur's bridle near the bit, Benjy murmured, "And now I shall lose the last friend I have left," into the horse's twitching ear.

Marion was pacing up and down in a small open place that looked down the slight rise of river bank to the rushing, dark water below.

"Ah, yes, young Master Brant," the colonel said when Benjy pulled his forelock politely in salute. "I have now heard your full story from Captain Lind who is returned." Benjy nodded that he knew. "A sad story it is, too, but I believe you acted prudently yourself. Also you have been of much help to me in this matter of Tarleton's Legion. Why do you wish to see me?"

"Because, Colonel, suh, of what Lieutenant DuMonseau said as he lay dying. I do not understand it, but you may. He said to give you his horse and then his voice fell away with the weakness, suh, and I did not catch every word. But it sounded like," he began to repeat what he remembered, " 'look . . . seek . . . saddle . . . and give . . . to . . . promise . . . give to . . . Marion only' and so I am come to you, suh, wi' horse and saddle."

"And did you examine the saddle? D'ye suppose he had some secret information there?"

"The British had the horse and Antoine knew they had it, yet he said what I have told you. I studied on the saddle in every way and could discover nothing, Colonel, no more than a bit of hominy and corn in the pockets and some flint and steel and bandages. I took the saddle all off and turned it around. I could find no secret any place. Would you examine it yourself, suh?"

"No, lad, no. I can but suppose that if 'twere anything of value, the enemy took it. Otherwise I'm sure the lieutenant meant nothing more than that I should have the disposal of the horse. And that I should decide that the recipient of the animal gets the saddle. So be it." Brushing back his straight hair from his temples, the colonel turned to his nephew. "Gabriel, send for my staff officers to this spot, quick now."

Benjy made a gesture toward tethering Monsieur at a nearby sapling and the colonel did not stay him, but he did signify for the boy to remain. "Wait," he said, as the officers began to gather, "for this concerns you."

Benjy could not imagine how unless it were to see the disposition of Monsieur. Lucky the man who received him, the boy thought. Presently, the officers were gathered and stood round in a semicircle. Colonel Marion walked into the middle and turned to his servant who was tending a small fire nearby.

"Oscar," said Colonel Marion, "bring me that horse."

Benjy felt a lump rise in his throat; surely, the colonel might have let him lead Monsieur to his new master? Marion spoke again.

"We have with us as you see, gentlemen, this young man who first alerted me to the danger of Colonel Tarleton's arrival by his sharp observations during a most poignant and difficult episode in his young life. Thus was I prepared even before the report of Captain Richardson and was able to make my plans ahead, as I much prefer to do ever. Here we rest now safe and sound in a secure position. My thanks, and it gives me some pleasure to reward you, Master Benjamin Brant, with a horse to replace your father's that you have lost in our service. This be one you have rid with your friend that owned him and which you will therefore cherish. Come forward, boy."

Benjy understood at last about the little formation and

his cheeks burned red with surprise, joy, even a bit of fright.

"I . . . I fear me I don't deserve such a gift, Colonel, suh," he stammered, "he were meant for such as you yourself."

"I know, I know, but I have made my disposition. Here, take the bridle with a firm hand, don't tremble," the colonel said. His black eyes twinkled.

Benjy took the bridle; all the officers raised their voices in a "huzzah for young Brant!" and he flushed again in pride and excitement.

Yet his pleasure did not endure long. At supper time Captain Lind sought him out to share baked sweet potatoes and soup with him.

"Go to bed," he advised as soon as they had cleared away the remains of the meal. "For we shall leave at daybreak."

"The troop?" Benjy asked timidly. The captain had not yet smiled at him and had not said one kind word about Monsieur, though other officers had clapped his shoulders and wished him well.

"No, you and I. I've an errand toward Rugeley's mills to determine the whereabouts of our army under General Harrington, and 'twill take me close enough to put you toward home," the captain announced.

Benjy stared at him. "I'm to go home?" he whispered then.

"Aye."

"Why? Why? Have I done so poor as to be dismissed?" The boy did not want to ask that but felt that he must.

"I would send you home," Captain Lind replied firmly.

"You don't want me with you?" his voice went thin, pleading.

"I have not said that; but you will remember that I wanted you not to begin with. Time has not improved you much. You know not the meaning of patriotism nor the color of honor."

"I do! I do!" the boy protested. "You are wicked and unkind and I hate you!" Coming on a short run, Benjy kicked Captain Lind in the right shin with all his strength. "I hate you! I hate you and so did Antoine!"

The captain simply reached out and caught the boy's left wrist and then his right one in an easy sweeping motion of his own right hand. He was powerful enough to lift the boy off his feet. "Say that again," he commanded.

"He . . . he . . . didn't . . . I guess," Benjy admitted.

"You know," the captain said and released him.

"I'm sorry . . ." Benjy managed to squeeze out an apology.

But Captain Lind shook his head. "No, you're not. You're afraid of me. That's not the same thing. You ran away to your adventure and you may run back now and remember it. You're not ready to soldier for your country, boy; you're not quite man enough. Now let's have an end to it."

Benjy dropped his head. He had descended from an honor he had never expected into a shame that wrenched his heart. He went slowly to find his bit of torn blanket. Sitting down to sulk, he realized that much of what the captain had said was true. He was too quick to be hurt, too quick with his feelings, and he was afraid . . . And though the captain had not said so, surely he knew, as Benjy himself knew, that what he had done for Colonel Marion, was a result of sheer luck . . . he had risked nothing . . . and lost nothing . . .

CHAPTER TWENTY-ONE

Of Stitches and Honesty

THE MORNING came in as drab as undyed wool. Benjy had slept badly. His hands and feet seemed weighted with lead. He dragged everlastingly over watering Monsieur and Hamlet down at the river edge. Coming back, he found Captain Lind talking to Major Peter Horry. The captain's saddlebags were all packed and waiting. Benjy hustled to roll up his piece of blanket. He thought bitterly that all he should have to take back to his father was what had been Antoine's. He had lost two rifles and their Bessie . . . A heavy hand touched his shoulder.

"You stay," said Captain Lind. "By the colonel's orders. I must go alone and on somewhat more complicated business. Do you behave well in my absence, since I be yet charged wi' you. Good luck, and I thank you . . . for these," he held out both his hands a moment in a simple gesture of gratitude.

Benjy was touched by the captain's graciousness and by his reprieve. Was it sheer accident because of the captain's assignment or had Colonel Marion spoken kindly for him? He knew that he could not find out. Suddenly, he realized that it would have been much easier to go home. In a minute, he would be entirely alone among men to whom his name was scarcely known. He looked up into Lind's eyes, overwhelmed.

"I am not to go home?" he asked.

"No, you will stay. You must report yourself to Major Horry in my absence," the captain said.

"Shall you be back soon, suh?" Benjy was anxious under the spur of coming loneliness.

Captain Lind smiled a brief smile, the first warmth he had shown since he had learned of Antoine's death. "I trust so," he said. Grasping the pommel of Hamlet's saddle and the reins, the captain mounted.

Too quickly he was gone between two trees down the path to the river. Benjy spent the loneliest day of his life then. He was too shy to seek out the company of the younger boys like Gwinn and Goddard and William Dobein James. He kept to himself, brooding. And all the day long, even into early dusk, small groups of men or single scouts kept going and coming. The colonel must be scouring the neighborhood for news, Benjy thought, or planning something. Not every party came in unscathed. Two men had buckshot to pick out of their legs, for they had come too close to a Tory farmer; another had a saber cut from a clash with a lighthorse expressman. Marion needed to find out exactly what had happened to Tarleton and what steps the British in Camden and Charlestown were taking to combat his own growing reputation.

After sharing a supper of salt pork and sweet potatoes with two men from the upper country, Benjy curled up at full dark and fixed his head in his arms for sleeping. He had not quite drifted off when shouting and scuffling disturbed him, followed by a lot of talk. Several torches flared.

The boy sat up. Five or six men bore in a fellow on an uncured cowhide. One of the younger lieutenants, as white as milk in the torchlight, had a long wound in his left thigh, deeper than Will Brant's had been and as long as the one

Antoine had received at the Waxhaws. From the talk that rolled about the group, the young man had been knifed by a British scout.

"He be bleedin' to death," someone observed.

"No, he not," another said, "but it be necessary for someun' to keep it clamped shut so it knits."

Thus began a vigil typical of the brotherliness that existed in Colonel Marion's troop. Benjy and two others volunteered to sit with the wounded man and hold the lips of the wound together until they knit. When the one holding felt his fingers getting numb, he called another to spell him. In the morning, another man joined the group making the time span shorter for each. Colonel Marion came to look upon the wounded soldier at mid-morning.

"Suh, where be the young surgeon that tended my father? The one who were wi' ye after the battle of King's Mountain when Captain Lind was first rounding up men?" Benjy asked the colonel. It was a question he had long meant to ask Lind. During the boy's service with the partisan troop, Marion had never had a surgeon. In fact, he had just written General Harrington about his need for one.

"Haldon Wartley?" the colonel asked. The boy nodded. "Ah, that's a tale I like not to have to tell you, boy; he was hanged."

"Hanged?"

"Yes, in an act of vengeance! His father, also a surgeon, had cared for the wounded of both sides at the siege of Charlestown," the colonel said; Benjy remembered the young doctor and the prisoners from the Mountain. "You might not understand, young Brant, how in these times a Whig can also murder a Whig? But thus was Hal Wartley hanged by his own side."

Benjy shuddered. He had thought of the young doctor

during Antoine's suffering, wondering if he could have done more than the British surgeon. So Wartley had died first! Though Benjy's shoulders ached sometimes during his vigils throughout the day, he never sought relief from the task he had accepted. Carefully, he took his turn holding the wound edges together. The patient became conscious after a while and took a little brandy from someone's precious bottle. Later, they fed him corn mush and molasses.

Benjy was having his turn at the wound late that afternoon when someone came through the brush seeking him.

"Benjamin Brant? Be he hereabout?"

Benjy called out. A second later, he shouted for his relief partner. As soon as he could release his hold upon the wound, he jumped up and ran across a short open space. Will Brant had come between the trees and stood, waiting. They did not speak at the moment of reunion, father and son. But Will looked upon a boy grown half a head taller. He smiled. Then they set about walking, beside each other, in a little circle round and round. As if the motion set their tongues going, they asked each other questions and gave each other answers. Bettina's lambs had grown; the sheep from Hawley were doing well; the winter vegetables were all in and stored; Will Brant could ride now and had only a slight limp when he walked; no weaving could be done that winter so he had come to serve with Colonel Marion at that dark time when men were so desperately needed. Yes, Striker had got home safely; Moomoo was fine; so were Melly and Maw. Alice Hawley was become a young lady, wearing her curls bound up under a cap. On his part, Benjy told his adventures and about the death of Antoine. He asked if Captain Lind had stopped at Cheraw on his present assignment. But he had not; Will Brant had come to keep his word.

"What did you think, Paw, when I ran off and Striker came back alone?" Benjy finally ventured to ask.

"Why, I thought 'let him go' if his time is come early. For the time always comes when the chick spreads its wings and flies into the pecan tree, when the duckling discovers that its feet are webbed and takes to the pond," Will Brant smiled the quiet smile that Benjy had seldom appreciated before.

While they talked, Mr. Brant also took a turn at holding the young lieutenant's wound closed. He shook his head at the great gash. "Why have ye not tried to put stitching in't?" he asked.

"No one knows how to," a man replied.

"When Dr. Wartley sewed up my leg, see here," Mr. Brant dropped down his one legging, "he did a right fancy stitching from side to side, under and out, as the women quilt. You can yet see the scarring where the stitches lay. But he told me any stitching, though clumsy, be better than none in a wound like this, so deep and wide. Mine was let go three days too long and I be lucky not to ha' lost my leg. He said any man might take a farrier's needle and boil a bit of sinew to soften it."

"Do it then!" the lieutenant spoke up bravely. "Do it and relieve us all of this agony of holding. Should trouble arise, I cannot take four men from their duty."

So Will Brant did a bit of rough surgery, using simple stitches that he tied off individually. As soon as he had finished and they had made the lieutenant comfortable under a packing of wet tow, which could now be kept upon the closed wound, Mr. Brant had to explain what he had done to a widening circle of the curious. At the same time he had to exhibit the scars on his thigh made by Dr. Wartley's fancy professional job.

All this while Benjy waited to get his father back so they could talk again privately. He remembered now that he had not told about receiving Monsieur or even about Antoine's curious directions about the saddle. In fact, the business of the surgical stitching recalled the saddle to Benjy's mind. The only decoration on the good leather saddle was stitching. In almost the same quilting stitch that the young surgeon had used on Will Brant's leg, over and under and back, and over and under and back, the saddle had a stacked circle design on both side housings of the seat. Curiously, no decoration appeared anywhere else on the saddle, not on skirt or shallow fender. Benjy traced the quilting pattern; it descended from one circle to two, three, four, and five.

Suppertime came and curtailed Mr. Brant's tales. Even the lieutenant ate broth and corn pone. Afterward, Benjy succeeded in retrieving his father. Will Brant listened carefully to Antoine's cryptic message. He immediately asked to see the saddle which Benjy brought and set on a stump.

"When you were talking about your stitch marks, I remembered these circles," Benjy said. "Would they mean anything?"

"Why, I don't know; your uncle had a fine saddle with stitching upon it. But surely, we can find out. Could your lieutenant have said: 'Look, see. . . *in* the saddle'?" Mr. Brant wondered. "These scrolls could be just fancy work but it seems to me that they are oddly the right size to contain coins . . . "

"I never thought of that," Benjy ran a finger over the top circle; but the saddle was thick leather on both sides.

"We shall have to open the housing edge here at the bottom and cut the stitching on the bottom row to see," his father said.

They took the saddle into a sheltered spot and Will Brant found a lighted pine knot to see by. Carefully, with the point of his hunting knife, Benjy's father cut the stitches that bound the two pieces of the housing together. Then he attacked the row of five circles and released the quilting stitch around the first bottom half. Sure enough, within moments a heavy coin was revealed, held yet secure in the remaining half of quilted circle. Before long, they knew that Antoine DuMonseau had been carrying thirty gold guineas in his saddle. Mr. Brant looked keenly at his son in the flickering light of the pine knot.

"All this money be yours, my son," he said, "since the colonel gave you horse and accoutrements." He watched the boy's face shrewdly. "You might replace our entire lost flock with such gold today."

Benjy stared up at him. "Oh, it is not my money!" he cried. "I could never claim it. Antoine said over and over: 'give . . . to Marion . . . only . . . ' He meant for the colonel to have it for his brigade, I know . . . "

His father clapped him hard and approvingly on the shoulder. "Good, my son!" he said. "So you told me from the beginning, not knowing what 'twas; I thank God you think right on such a thing. Forgi' me for tempting you; but when a duckling takes to the water, it cannot always swim." He made this speech gently but with pride. "Let us take the coins out carefully, and you may carry them to the colonel. And later on, we can put the stitching back so no one will ever know it was removed."

CHAPTER TWENTY-TWO

Of a Mission Accomplished

FROM HIS safe place at Benbow's Ferry, Colonel Marion began scouring the Williamsburg district for several weeks. Then he made an unsuccessful attempt upon Georgetown. About this time scouts brought in the story about Tarleton saying when he left the Ox Swamp area: "Come along, boys, and let's find the Gamecock (Sumpter), as for that demmed old fox, Marion, the devil himself couldn't catch him." Tories and patriots alike soon added "swamp" to "fox" and thus gave the little colonel the nickname that was to be his forever.

Other matters were not so amusing. During the Georgetown expedition Marion's nephew Gabriel was killed; report had Tarleton clashing with Sumpter at Blackstock and the American commander seriously wounded; Marion's numbers dwindled daily as his men went home, with or without leave as the spirit moved them, to set their homes in order for winter, to smoke their meat, to harvest their late crops. In all this time nothing was heard from Captain Lind. Benjy was glad to have his father in and out of camp on various errands. Sometimes the boy went along; sometimes, as on the affair at Georgetown, he was left behind.

Word came down, too, that Wemyss had got his comeuppance, having been both wounded and captured. Finally, most serious to Colonel Marion was the news that both Balfour in Charlestown and Lord Rawdon in Camden were sending detachments of militia, volunteers, and regulars to hem him in.

As the roads began to swarm with detachments of soldiers and militia, it was evident that the communication about the two British garrison commanders and their collaboration was only too true. Marion went into bivouac on the bluff rising above the western bank of the Peedee River. From here he continued to despatch his scouts and often he had distressing casualties. One bright morning in late November, he sent for his staff. "I must have more detailed knowledge of what British detachments and troops be on road," he said. "If we could send someone out in daylight?"

"Why not a boy like Gwinn or Brant, alone?" one of his captains suggested. "A boy on mule wi' a string of pelts to trade would be less suspect than anyone."

So Benjy was chosen to ride up toward Kingstree by way of Lower Bridge and the river road to check on the rumor that the 64th Regiment under Major McLeroth was approaching Kingstree to set up a post there. As he made ready to get astride the mule someone had provided, along with a string of beaver pelts and a web of brown wool his father had brought, Benjy felt his father's hand upon his shoulder.

"My son, be wary, and hear some good Scots counsel that I should have gi' you before this: be slow to speak and to anger; be quick to see danger and to choose the right; and deliberate on all else."

"Yes, Father," he said solemnly, impressed with the seriousness of his mission.

In the crispness of a new morning, the boy set off. His first day on road brought him no information. He stopped at a small tavern. There a Tory militiaman talked of shifting British troops but named no names or units. He had skipped off from the mounted infantry of a Captain Coffin with a good horse and didn't seem anxious to go back. Benjy paid for his lodging and supper with two of his beaver skins. Not much traffic along the road, except by the generally non-paying military, made innkeepers glad of anything they could get.

The next morning, the river was running high. At Mobayin, it flooded the road. Just before noon Benjy rode into a place known to be patriot. To his surprise the house was abandoned and the barns had been razed—perhaps during one of Tarleton's raids or vengeance rides? Every Whig in the neighborhood seemed to be in hiding. Loneliness struck at the boy with each additional mile the mule covered. At length he put on a bold front and whistled gaily to cover his distress.

To his dismay, a British patrol of four horsemen rode out of an unexpected brush-covered lane. Two were redcoated and two green. For a terrible moment or two, Benjy supposed the green-jacketed men to be Tarleton's. Had the British Legion again descended below Camden? But the men spoke brokenly and Benjy soon realized that they were Hessians. One of the redcoats merely asked the boy a few questions. Where was he from, they wanted to know; and he replied that he was from the hill country. Did he go armed? He made no attempt to deny the rifle looped into a saddle strap. He produced his skins to show why he was armed. The Germans took one of the skins and babbled about it gutturally. Then one of the Loyalist troopers explained, "He wants to keep your skin and let you go along. Is it all right?"

Better the beaver skin than his own, Benjy thought, and

agreed smiling. He resumed his whistling as he continued on his way. At least, he whistled until he had left them out of sight. Then he was more careful. It was not cold; the countryside was drab but unfrozen. Benjy was sorry to see the sun set. Near Doyley's an old man told him that the eastern side of the great Trading Road "weltered wi' British soldiers." How long would it be quiet and lonely on the road to Kingstree?

For a long while, Benjy passed nothing at all, no plantation house, no cabin, no farm or barn. He munched hardtack from his saddlebag and kept kicking the mule with both heels. Shivering more from tension than cold, Benjy kept on into the dark of full night. Once in a while he had to reach the mule a coaxing handful of oats. Finally, between Woods' and Weatherspoon's, he saw the welcome light of a small inn. It seemed deserted; no horse stood at the hitching post. Its sign, a dilapidated partridge, hung by one hinge whining in the thin breeze. Still holding the mule's lead, Benjy knocked at the door.

An old woman pulled the door in. She held a candle in a pewter holder. "Have ye money to pay?" she asked suspiciously.

Benjy considered that he surely didn't look like a marauder. But perhaps the poor woman had once been deceived by just such a boy as he. She was not much softened by his reply that he had "nice beaver skins and a web o' wool." She opened the door wider begrudgingly. Then, noticing the mule, she told Benjy to take it into a shed behind.

Benjy found the shelter directly and noticed again that no other animals were about except a weather-beaten cow that needed milking. He offered to milk her for his supper. The old woman accepted. When Benjy set the pail of warm milk in the open kitchen, the crone handed him a bowl of hot stew. It was mostly turnips and carrots with just a smidgeon of beef; but to the hungry boy, it seemed delicious compared with the dried cow peas, pone, and hominy of road fare. The old woman let him dipper out a mug of clabber from the day before and then ushered him into the great room which was sooty from a smoking hickory log and only dimly lit with two thick candles.

In a corner another guest hunched over his plate of stew. Benjy looked toward him with casual curiosity. Then he looked again, more carefully. The man was big by the line of his shoulders, poorly dressed in dirty torn buckskin with a skin breech clout and Indian type leggings, moccasins, and between them a wrapping of burlap or tow against wet and cold. The fellow sopped his stew noisily and paid the boy no heed at all. Yet from time to time, Benjy was pushed to look across at him. Something seemed familiar about the line of his body. Curious, Benjy had one mind to go to bed and another to sit a while.

A jngle of arms and a rat-a-tat at the door presently decided for him. The old woman grumbled loudly about "violent times and murderin' horsemen" and went to see. A troop of soldiers roared in noisily, all but shoving her aside. They called out, "Serve us, b'gad! and be quick!" They were all red-coated with buff trousers; all were under arms. A lieutenant and a cornet evidently kept them in order because they soon sprawled out around two tables and managed not to bellow too much; especially after the lieutenant promoted their cause with the old woman by ordering a couple of gallons of cider.

Upon its delivery, the lieutenant went to the man in the corner and clapped him on the shoulder. Pulling up a stool, he sat upon it and asked, "Well, John, and what's your news?"

"Up and down between the ferries and in goodly number," the man replied.

Benjy almost yelped for he knew the voice as he had almost known the shape and form. He suspected, too, that the message was in reference to that foxy Colonel Marion. Afraid some regular had seen his start of surprise, Benjy knocked over *his* stool as though he had got up awkwardly. Of course, everyone in the room looked toward him, including the old woman.

"How now, Grandmother, company?" asked the lieutenant. "I thought we told you to mind what you took in this night."

" 'Tis but a back-country boy wi' some skins to sell," she growled.

"Harris, go see what's out back," the lieutenant ordered one man. Then he looked full at Benjy. "Come here," he said. And as he gave the command, Benjy knew him, too, as swiftly as he had recognized the voice of David Lind in the bearded, buck-skinned stranger who now faced him fully. The lieutenant was the one who had frightened him so at Congers and given him the sixpence for his rifle. The very sixpence lay beneath his fingers in his right breeches pocket, for he had always transferred it from one set of clothes to another to mind him not to be foolhardy. Thank heaven, he had not been so stupid as to blurt out his recognition of Captain Lind; and in the same breath, he prayed a quick prayer that the lieutenant would never expect to find him in that tavern that night. He prayed as he came reluctantly across the space between. He avoided the lieutenant's eyes and looked, instead, at Lind's. Not a flicker of notice was on the straight face of the erstwhile captain, not a glimmer of friendliness or any recognition in the steel-blue eyes. Indeed, Lind was bearded the full month's growth of his absence; his reddish curls were greasy and filthy. He seemed surprisingly ill-armed, all Benjy could see was a sheathed hunting knife at his belt. But then Lind knew dozens of tricks for hiding pistols and knives. But where was his horse? And was he a parolee of the British, a complacent prisoner, or the informer he had just sounded?

"Come closer, boy, for methinks there is that about you I've seen before," the lieutenant said.

Benjy had to look at him. He hoped his glance was firm. The young officer stared, then wrinkled his mouth into a half sneer. "Aha! Did I not tell you once that I never forget a face, heh?" he roared. "Have ye yet the sixpence Bertie paid ye for your rifle, heh? Speak, boy!"

Benjy bluffed. "You mistake me, suh," he said, but the *s* slurred.

"Not I, not Charles Welles. You're to do wi' sheep somewhere when I was wi' Major Wemyss, and I doubt not I can smell the sheep manure about ye," he reached out a long arm and pulled the boy to him by the fringe at his neck. "Damme! Don't lie to me, boy. Did I not gi' you sixpence to get off wi' ye, one night last fall?"

"No! I never saw you before," Benjy cried as hotly as he could, too vehemently perhaps.

The lieutenant threw back his right arm and slammed his palm across the boy's cheeks, first backhanded and then palmed. Tears ran out of Benjy's eyes.

"Answer me," Welles shouted.

"I don't know you," the boy insisted. Swiftly, he was struck again, two blows that made his nose bleed and his mouth also, inside. He swallowed the salty taste of his own blood.

"Search him," the lieutenant then ordered.

The ensign nodded to two of the soldiers who did a

thorough job. First, they wrenched Benjy's hands behind him. One lifted him and the other pulled off his shoepacks. Then they tore off his hunting shirt and stripped down his breeches. While the boy stood shivering, naked except for his tow shift, the soldiers shook out his clothes and down fell the telltale sixpence on the floor, of course, and nothing more than his penknife and six shillings his father had spared him against need. All of this, Lind watched with cool calm and made never a movement for or against.

"Now then," the lieutenant laughed and held the sixpence between thumb and forefinger. "Did I not give it ye in the upper country?"

Benjy whispered, "Yes," and hung his head. The great room rocked with laughter at his admission.

"Now take him outside and condition him a little wi' a stick, so he knows what to expect when we question him," the lieutenant seemed mightily amused, and his men with him.

Captain Lind stood sober as stone. The men who had stripped Benjy dragged him out-of-doors. While one held his head in a vise-like grip under his arm, the other beat him soundly with a birch branch. The boy ground his teeth together and thought of his father the night the surgeon had come. He never murmured. Since they could get neither howl nor curse from him, the two soldiers found no sport in their task and soon desisted. One gave Benjy his trousers and shoepacks to put on and shoved him limping into the tavern again.

Lieutenant Welles then threw the sixpence on the dirt floor between them and said, "Pick it up!" as he had that night at Congers. How long ago that seemed and yet the humiliation was immediately the same. Benjy bent with some difficulty to obey, seeing no way out of it. The officer tripped him. Laughter waved over his prone figure like a tide. In very spite, he bit his lower lip. Then painfully, he retrieved the token of his misery and struggled to his knees. Behind the lieutenant, even Lind grinned openly now. Benjy riled; then he remembered his father's counsel and he began to think it over and over to himself: "Be slow to speak and to anger; be quick to see danger and to choose the right; and deliberate on all else." Thinking became a comfort against his multiple hurts inside and out. The laughter died away. The lieutenant went to have a swig of cider.

During this interim Harris came in with Benjy's saddlebags, the pelts, and the roll of wool. The ensign glanced through the saddlebags and, finding nothing of use or interest, left them on a chair. The beaver skins the soldiers tossed about for a while as though they were bean bags, and the wool they rolled out and flipped in waves and draped upon themselves like a Roman toga, dirtying it. Tiring of this byplay they soon kicked both items into a corner where the old crone kept a cagey eye upon them. She could certainly clean up the wool; good wool was not easily come by. The fur, too, would be useful.

Presently, Lieutenant Welles spoke again, directly to Benjy. "Now, boy, before I toss your present rifle to Harris there for another sixpence . . . " this proposal was greeted with loud laughter, of course . . . "you may take your oath for your sovereign, and mayhap we'll let you go on your way wi' no more punishment."

At this David Lind kicked back his stool and came to stand at the head of a table where four soldiers were laying their cards in a round of faro. Benjy cast one even look in the captain's direction and got no recognition; he was not sure he had expected any.

The lieutenant recalled his attention sharply. "So, will you state your name and that you swear by King George to be a true subject and not bear arms against your rightful governors?"

"I be Benjamin Brant of Cheraw township and I be for Carolina and may his Majesty George the Third roast in hell!" He said it all of a piece and as boldly as he might have kissed Alice Hawley under a maypole. And he lunged forward and kicked Lieutenant Welles with all his force first with one shoepack edge and then the other beneath the officer's right kneecap.

The soldiery stared for several seconds in stunned silence until the lieutenant shrieked in pain. Then the ensign came to his senses and struck Benjy from behind with the butt of a rifle, knocking him to the floor.

Benjy came around with his ears buzzing; and he could not move at all. It took him several moments to realize that he was bound by his hands to the legs of a table across which he lay on his back full length. Things were quiet. He lay agonizingly still, not sure that he had any use of his legs and afraid to open his eyes. He did open them finally. Some of the soldiers must have gone out but four still played cards on Benjy's right. Also within range of his vision to the right was Lieutenant Welles bathing his bruised leg in a bucket of hot water the old crone had supplied.

The old innkeeper jangled silver under her apron. Lind made charcoal marks on a map at Benjy's left to the obvious interest of Lieutenant Welles' ensign. Benjy's head hurt where the ensign had knocked him from behind, and his arms ached from their uncomfortable posture. Gingerly, he tested his left leg and found it free; so he soon discovered was the right one, but he could not move without attracting attention. The slightest twist would roll him off the narrow table and into an even more miserable position. How long he could endure the mounting torment of his situation, he dared not imagine. What were they going to do with him for his boldness? He blinked a few times and was glad the candles were not too bright. He could not tell what bound his wrists but it was secure enough.

Presently, the old woman took her pewter candlestick and candle and went up a rickety stair at the far left of the room to a chamber above. Almost as if this had been a signal, Captain Lind folded up the map. But then he just sauntered lazily around the card players, past the lieutenant who still nursed his leg and over to the soldier posted at the door as a guard; finally he came back to Benjy. He snapped his thumb and middle finger on Benjy's forehead hard enough to make the boy gasp.

"And are ye for King George yet, boy?" he asked.

And Benjy answered, "No, never!" hotly before he realized that by some adroit movement of one hand, Lind had freed him from the table leg and was standing before his hands rubbing his wrists to renew their circulation with one hand while with the other he was twisting and turning the good Brant wool about him and making antics with his legs like a highland dancer. A couple of the card players giggled; the sentry at the door reached out a helpful foot to disentangle the last few feet of material from where it had caught on a stool.

A second later, the candle on the card table tipped, spilling hot wax and disconcerting the players. The sentry went out the door backwards under propulsion from the captain's wicked left fist. Benjy felt himself propelled up under the back of his neck; a British cavalry carbine was thrust into his hand. He brought it to bear valiantly upon the card players while Captain Lind laid out the ensign and drew a pistol on the lieutenant.

"Open your mouth and I'll kill you," Lind told Welles firmly but quietly; then he ordered one of the soldiers to gag the lieutenant and tie his hands behind his back and then to do the same for each of his fellow soldiers. The ensign and the sentry were as quiet as death and would likely be for half an hour, Benjy knew. As the moments flew by, he felt warmer and more comfortable. Finally, Captain Lind had no trouble at all in persuading the last soldier, after he was divested of arms and boots, to run lickety-split up the highway without looking back.

Then Lind stood outside and put his fingers to his lips in a familiar whistle. Very shortly, a clatter of hooves responded and Hamlet tore out of the swamp across the road on the river side and stood waiting.

Benjy got on his shirt, gathered up his saddlebags, his wool, and even his remaining beaver skins for the old woman had had enough from the enemy. Captain Lind burned the map in the fireplace and then, pausing before the bound lieutenant, took up the bucket in which Welles had been soaking his leg.

"Since you enjoy humiliation, my fair friend, here's to you; and mind that I told you no lie when I said Marion's men were up and down between the ferries. With my commander's compliments and mine!" and he upset the bucket over the lieutenant's powdered head.

A moment later, the captain and the boy were off on the big stallion, Lind's strong arm about the boy's waist. For an hour they rode at a hard gallop, until they had crossed Lower Bridge and taken the southern road. Then Captain Lind found a sturdy oak in a scrub field and set Hamlet to rest bridleless and laid out their blankets.

"I be not finished with my mission," Benjy said, first thing, and told how he had been sent to discover what was happening at Kingstree.

"I have enough information so that Colonel Marion can safely attack this McLeroth and rid us of him," the captain assured him.

So then Benjy told how his father had come to join the brigade and how he had discovered the coins in the saddle and how graciously Colonel Marion had received them and how he had given one to Benjy to keep in memory of the dead lieutenant.

" 'Tis good I left it wi' my paw," the boy said, feeling for the sixpence in his trousers pocket.

"Aye." The captain agreed.

"I would I had done better what I was sent to do," Benjy repeated. "I have lost the mule. I am forever losing something valuable and gaining nothing . . . "

"Your country has gained you at long last, boy, know you not that? No mission be more important or better accomplished than the one you have done this night which has made you a man of honor in the name of liberty and Carolina," Captain Lind said.

Benjy looked at him in the starlight. "You think that?" he asked, and he was somehow choked with many feelings.

"I do." The captain extended his hand and the boy grasped it in both of his.

And again Benjy separated the sixpence from the shillings in his pocket and somehow it was a different symbol, not of humiliation but of triumph.